Praise for
Divine Intervention

"*The Dining and Social Club for Time Travellers* is full of fantasy and will be enjoyed by young readers who like oddball characters and time-travelling adventures."

—Erin Stewart, **TRIBUTE MAGAZINE**

"A clever, original story that dances with life from page one. Hilarious and heartbreaking, this is a book that will spark the imagination of children and adults around the world."

—Robin Spano, Author of *The Dead Politician Society series*

"*Divine Intervention* is an action-packed and often laugh-out-loud tale peopled with the best kind of quirky characters. The series has kicked off with a brilliant bang, and I can't wait to find out what happens to its heroine, Louisa, next!"

—Maeve O'Regan, **INTERNATIONAL FESTIVAL OF AUTHORS**

"*Divine Intervention* is a powerful saga highly recommended for young adult and adult readers alike."

—Diane Donovan, *Donovan's Literary Service*

"**One of the best YA titles of 2016!** Written in an earnest, amusing style, the novel delivers a tale of friendship, family and fate that is sure to please, offering a refreshing new take on the rules and consequences of time travelling."

—Stephanie Bucklin, **FOREWORD MAGAZINE**

DIVINE INTERVENTION

ELYSE
KISHIMOTO

Author, Elyse Kishimoto
Co-author and illustrator, Doug Feaver
Cover artist, Nacho Yagüe

Cataloging-in-Publishing Data has been applied for and may be obtained from Library and Archives Canada.

ISBN 978-0-9940897-1-7

Second edition, printed and bound by Friesens Press, Altona, MB, CAN
Distributed by Fitzhenry and Whiteside Ltd., Markham, ON, CAN
Published in 2016 by Green Jellybean Press, Toronto
www.greenjellybeanpress.com

www.thetimetravellersclub.com

To Donna

The Time Travellers

Louisa Sparks
21st century, England

Harold
17th century, Denmark

Adalbert Uhrmacher
16th century, Germany

Brünnhilde
17th century, Denmark

Gendun
21st century, France

Rhadamanthus Finch
16th century, England

Edward Krunk
20th century, United States

Theoderic
9th century, Norway

Alpharabius
13th century, Iraq

Radicon Spring
23rd century, England

Belthazzar
Origin unknown

The Nephilim
Origin unknown

Sigermus
10th century, Ireland

Amog
Alternate dimension

Rogvolod
19th century, Russia

Leonardo da Vinci
15th century, Italy

"'Tis oft' the smallest alterations giveth rise to strikingly great consequences."

-Rhadamanthus Finch

Contents

PROLOGUE

IT TAKES a keen eye to spot a time traveller. The members of this secret society go to extraordinary lengths not to attract any attention, but it is hard to remember everything. Despite their best efforts, they are always leaving clues. It might be a ticket stub from a train that no longer runs or the cut of a suit that is decades out of fashion. Maybe it is a hat or a pair of sunglasses or even a moustache that doesn't quite belong. It could be a single gesture or word that fell from use centuries ago or as small a thing as a green jellybean in the palm of a hand. Time travellers are always eating green jellybeans. If you are lucky enough to spot a time traveller, you should be careful not to raise any suspicions, or he will be gone in a flash.

Telling a tale about time travellers is a complicated matter, full of twists and turns and sudden dead ends. It's hard to say where a story starts and where it finishes. Often, the beginning can turn out to be the end, and the end can be just the beginning. And it is usually the case that just when everything seems like it has been sorted out, the story gets infinitely more complicated.

How then do we begin our account? In the distance, we see the intricate web. Drawing closer we select a point. And then we start to follow the strand.

August 31st, 2012

The Village of Jardin,

Southern France

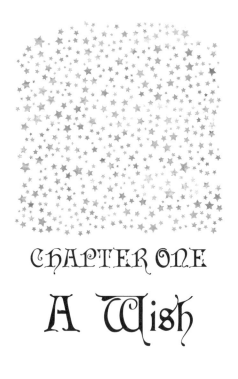

CHAPTER ONE

A Wish

IT HAD been four months since the night of the accident. Louisa Sparks gazed into the night sky from her tiny bedroom window in her grandfather's house. She counted the stars as they revealed themselves one by one. In London, where she used to live, there were only ever a few stars twinkling in the darkness. On most nights, it was easy to forget that they were there. But on a clear evening in her grandfather's village, the sky would turn to fire. A brilliant streak crossed the sky. She tried to make her wish clear and bright in her mind as she imagined it travelling up into space like a beam of white light.

The summer was nearing an end, and she was hardly sad anymore, at least not in the daytime when there were plenty of things to do in the village. She would often go to watch the men making wine. They would stand together in a big wooden bucket and squish the grapes with their bare feet. On sunny days, Louisa would ride her bicycle from one village to the next, along the wide gravel roads, past the fields of lavender and sunflowers. But when she was alone, and everything was quiet, thoughts of her parents would creep into her mind. After the accident, everything had changed. Without warning, she had been shut out of her old life. Her place in the world had become nothing but a memory.

Louisa's grandfather lived in the village of Jardin, in the south of France, along the border of Spain. His house was made of yellow stone and had an orange clay roof that was covered with green moss. He'd moved away from England long before Louisa was born and had not returned until the night of the accident. He had left England as a young man; he'd told her with a kind smile, and came back as an old one. Two weeks later, they returned to his home together.

Louisa, who could barely manage a few words under normal circumstances, hardly spoke to her grandfather at first. He was a stranger to her, someone with whom she shared only a vague connection. And Grandpa George, who was unaccustomed to having guests—especially ones of Louisa's age—also kept his distance during those early days. But slowly, things began to change.

Louisa turned from the window at the sound of scampering paws. Rosencrantz and Guildenstern had arrived. Rosencrantz, an old Basset Hound, greeted Louisa with a bark.

"And good evening to you, sir," she replied, doing her best impersonation of an old English gentleman.

Rosencrantz gave another bark.

"What is that you say, old chap? Oh yes, I do agree. 'Tis a fine evening for watching stars." Louisa rubbed behind the old hound's ears.

Guildenstern bumped Rosencrantz jealously.

"Stop grumbling, Guildenstern." Louisa scratched under the chubby brown Labrador's chin until he was panting happily.

The two dogs jumped onto her bed and settled themselves down into the covers. In no time, Rosencrantz was snoring, and Guildenstern was hunting a rabbit in his dreams. She could always tell when a rabbit was involved because he barked very quietly and wiggled his paws. Somehow it always made her feel safe when the dogs were sleeping.

Louisa climbed into her bed, twisting and turning to make a spot for herself. It was at these times when the activities of the day were over that she felt most lonesome, but tonight she was feeling downhearted for another reason. In two days, she would have to make an important decision: leave to attend school in Paris for the year, or stay with her grandfather and go to school in the village.

She picked up the brochure on her nightstand. The girl on the cover looked like a perfect little doll—just the type that belonged at Madame de Tréville's Preparatory School for Girls. Louisa puckered her lips like she'd tasted something sour. She would never fit in. Besides, over the summer, she had grown to adore her grandfather and the tiny village where he lived. Each day it was beginning to feel a little more like home. If she chose to go to Paris, everything would change again.

The next morning, she went to pick up some sweets for Grandpa George, even though he wasn't supposed to have them anymore. Each of the macarons was a different colour, and each one reminded her of something from her grandfather's village. The yellow was the golden field of sunflowers. The pink was the crumbling castle wall. The chocolate reminded her of the sandstone gargoyles that silently watched from their tower. The purple and blue were like the delicate flowers that grew in the tiered gardens of the monastery. The red was the row of snapdragons that lined the road to her grandfather's house. And the white reminded her of the butterflies that sat waiting on the leaves of the juniper bushes until she brushed past them and they floated into the air by the hundreds.

Louisa walked briskly up the winding cobblestone road towards her grandfather's house. She had finally decided where she would go to school but was feeling nervous about what her grandfather would say. She would have to wait for the perfect moment to tell him.

Louisa stopped to greet the little black cat sunning herself on the garden wall with her two front paws neatly crossed in front of her. "Hello, Ms. Nickels. You would miss me if I were to go to Paris, wouldn't you?" Louisa stroked Ms. Nickel's neck until the cat purred. "Who would scratch between your ears and rub your big fat belly?"

Grandpa George was waiting for Louisa at his gate with his kind smile and sun-darkened chin just visible beneath his shapeless straw hat. He had not aged like most men. Other than his wispy white hair, he looked like a man barely past the middle of his life. His eyes were bright, and his face was smooth, except for the faded scar that crossed his left cheek.

His face lit up when he saw Louisa skip up the lane towards him. "My, Louisa, you are the very image of your mother. You have the same dark red hair and sparkling blue eyes," he said with a faraway smile.

She opened the white box for her grandfather to see.

He made a deep, glad laugh, "Ah ha! What is this?" He picked a pastel blue crumb from Louisa's collar.

"You caught me!" Louisa blushed. There had been eight macarons, but she'd been unable to resist eating one.

They emerged from the house into the garden and Louisa clapped her hands when she saw the lavish feast that he had spent all day preparing. The food was laid out on a long wooden table underneath the canopy of the old oak tree. There were bowls of boiled potatoes and eggs, trays of grilled vegetables sprinkled with herbs from the garden, thick slices of chèvre and freshly baked bread. Grandpa George lifted the lid from a large clay pot, and the delicious aroma of cassoulet filled the air. In the centre of the table was a fluffy white cake decorated with twelve candles.

"Grandpa George, you remembered!"

"Forgive me, Louisa, I'm not much for gift wrapping." He held out his hand. "This locket has been passed on from mother to daughter for generations. It was to go to your mother, Margaret, but now it's yours to keep." He fastened it around Louisa's neck and stepped back.

"Thank you, Grandpa George. I will treasure it." The weight of it felt reassuring.

"Happy birthday, Louisa."

The corners of her eyes clouded with tears.

Grandpa George brushed away the big teardrop that had rolled down her cheek. "Now, now, my dearest girl, remember we made an agreement? No tears allowed."

She took a deep breath and turned to watch Rosencrantz and Guildenstern. Their noses were like two periscopes circling the table as they sniffed at the food. Louisa giggled. The dogs were getting quite chubby living with her grandfather.

Even the neighbour's duck wandered into the yard to investigate.

"You had better mind your manners, Monsieur Canard, or you will end up in my cassoulet!" Grandpa George warned.

The duck quacked and sat down, undeterred. Ms. Nickels was there too, hiding in the grass with her tail swishing in the air and her paws neatly folded in front of her.

Grandpa George sat on his wooden chair and placed his hat down beside him. He wiped the sweat from his forehead. The sun had been shining hot and bright. The sky was clear and blue, with only a few curls of cloud sitting very still amongst the tallest peaks far away in the distance. They spoke joyfully and ate until the warm day turned into a pleasant and fragrant evening.

"Grandpa George, I have something important to tell you." Louisa had waited long enough.

Grandpa George stood up from the table and paced. "Why, Louisa, I expect that you have made your decision and soon you will board a train," he said excitedly. "Not to worry, when you arrive in Paris, you shall forget about your doddering old grandfather and these two spoiled dogs."

"I won't forget," she promised. "But I hope you don't mind that I have decided to stay."

"Of course, I don't mind, sweet girl. There is nothing in the world that would make me happier."

Louisa detected a hint of concern in his voice. "I was afraid that you might say no—that you would want me to leave."

"Louisa, you have to do what feels right. You are always welcome here. Though, come fall, you may be wishing that you had left. Most of the other children will have gone away to school. I can still picture your mother when she was about your age, home for the holidays, pacing around here like a caged monkey."

"It's funny, but I can't remember mum ever mentioning where she went to school."

"Margaret graduated from Madame de Tréville's Preparatory School for Girls—with honours of course. Your Grandma Sophie and I were very proud."

"Did she like it there?"

"Very much so, yes. And your mother was also quite fond of Paris—too fond, perhaps." He gathered up the empty plates and took them inside. After he had cleared the table, Grandpa George set the needle on his old record player, and soft music filled the night air.

He arrived back in the garden with his pipe clenched in his teeth and a wool blanket in his hands, which he draped over Louisa's shoulders. The yellow lanterns hanging from the branches of the oak tree were lit. The dogs slept at Louisa's feet with bulging stomachs. The tiny black cat hid under the lilacs in the yard; the duck returned to his home and the night had become very still. For a long while, they sat in silence under the brilliant moon, set amongst an ocean of stars.

Tiny clouds of smoke rose from Grandpa George's pipe as he searched the night sky. The candlelight flickered and danced in his eyes. His cheeks, usually red as cherries, looked ghostly pale.

"Do you ever think about my parents?" Louisa asked.

"Always," he replied quietly.

"I miss them so much."

"I do too, Louisa."

∞

Later that evening, streaks of lightning crossed the sky, illuminating a vast cauldron of black clouds that had come tumbling out of the mountains. Each time the lightning flashed, the darkness lifted like a curtain. Thunder sounded with a *BOOM!* Rosencrantz and Guildenstern came scampering down the hallway. Two moist black noses poked up at the foot of Louisa's bed.

The silly dogs had two emotions—worry and happy—and they were constantly transitioning from one to the other. The two worried dogs leapt onto Louisa's bed and fell asleep at her feet, safe from the storm and happy once again.

Lightning flashed, and the whole village lit up as bright as day. Again the thunder sounded with a *BOOM!* Drops of rain spattered against the glass.

"Yikes!" Turquoise eyes flashed in the night. "Oh, it's just you." Louisa slipped out of her warm bed, crossed the room and opened the window. She scratched behind Ms. Nickels' ears, and the black cat began to purr. "Gross! You're wet!"

Rosencrantz gave a sharp bark and the skittish cat retreated onto the roof and then leapt over its edge. Ms. Nickel's stepped lightly across the top of the crumbling wall that bordered the yard. With another leap, the cat disappeared into the garden.

Again the lightning flashed and Louisa saw five

figures gathered together near the front gate. It was as if they had stepped out of the very air itself. Purple cloaks with deep hoods concealed their faces. One of them was quite obviously a child—she could tell by the slight frame that perhaps it was a young girl. One of the others glanced up at her and two blank discs gleamed from inside his hood. Louisa ducked below the window, drawing her knees up close to her thumping chest. *What on Earth?* Once more the lightning flashed, and the thunder sounded, shaking Grandpa George's little house. Louisa peeked up over the windowsill, but the five strangers were no longer on the road.

Louisa crept back into her bed and eventually fell into a restless sleep. She dreamt that she was standing in the yard of her old home. The garden was blooming with flowers, and the air was scented with bellflowers, primroses and violets. Warm light shone from the windows of the house. She was with her parents. They were alive! But the flowers in the garden wilted, and the light from inside of the house grew dim. Louisa watched helplessly as her parents' bodies turned to clay. "Mum, Dad." Her parents turned towards her, revealing gaping holes where their faces should have been.

Louisa awoke to the *tok! tok! tok!* of wood being chopped. She walked into the yard wrapped in her wool blanket. Her breath made tiny puffs in the crisp air.

The sun lifted over the horizon and the memory of her terrible dream faded with the moon and the twinkling stars into the purple sky. A fox with a mouse in her jaws stepped lightly across the yard; her red fur glistened in the pale morning light. The rain stopped, and everything was fresh and wet and cool.

Split by a lightning strike, the blackened halves of the old oak tree lay across the lawn with its branches piled in twisted heaps. Ms. Nickels' turquoise eyes peeked out at her from inside a tangle of branches. Grandpa George paused to wipe the sweat from his brow and then went back to work, his axe continuing its *tok! tok! tok!*

Louisa brushed her hand along the gate, feeling the cold droplets of rain that still clung to it. The smoky smell of wood and freshly baked bread drifted into the yard from the baker's ovens. The rooftops glowed orange in the red sun and the fields of sunflowers turned fiery gold. She glanced into the yard, thinking how gloomy it was, seeing the old oak broken to pieces. Louisa recalled what her mother used to say when something unexpected happened, "Nothing ever stays the same, my darling girl, no matter how much we wish it could." Although for Louisa, there had been too much change, too soon. Staying in the village was safe; she felt nothing bad could ever happen to her there. But, her mother's voice kept repeating in her mind.

She traced the rose pattern of the locket with her fingertip. She had not yet opened it, but it was time. Inside there was a faded photograph of her mother wearing her school uniform, standing at the gate of Grandpa George's house. Her eyes were lit with a sense of adventure—of possibility.

Louisa had been sure that she did not want to go to Paris, but something inside her had changed. She didn't know how to explain it exactly, but she sensed somehow that her time in the village was temporary. "I don't belong here," she said very quietly. Even though she adored her grandfather—Louisa knew that she could not stay.

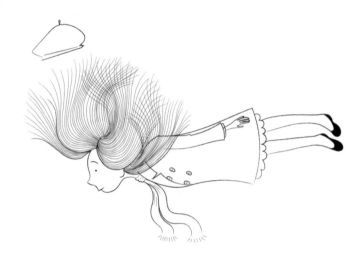

CHAPTER TWO

The Wormhole

GRANDPA GEORGE knelt at the foot of his wardrobe. He was looking for a matching pair of socks— preferably without holes. Instead, he found an old cigar box that he'd put there many years ago. He opened the lid hesitantly. Inside he found a photograph and a golden ring wrapped in purple silk. He lifted the picture.

"Good morning, Sophie darling," he said it as if she were sitting next to him. "Socks are what I am looking for," he muttered, snapping the box closed and returning it to its place. "Here we are." He poked his pinky finger through the heel. "Only one small hole."

He was about to close the doors of the wardrobe when he spotted an old coat of his neatly folded on the shelf. It was a navy blue peacoat with brass buttons, from when he was a boy. He could scarcely remember being so small, but he clearly recalled the day his father had brought it home. "Still in perfect shape," Grandpa George said aloud, beating the dust out of it with his palm.

He left his room and found Louisa sitting on her bed. He held the coat up for her to see. "Autumn in Paris is cold, and you will need a good sturdy jacket to keep you warm. Just a few minor adjustments and it will be as good as new."

Louisa slipped her arms into the coat and examined herself in the dressing mirror.

Grandpa George frowned. "What an old fool I am. You know Louisa, if we hurry, we can visit the shopkeeper and still make the train. I'd like to buy you a brand new coat, a proper one for a young lady who lives in Paris."

"No, Grandpa George, this one is perfect. I wouldn't want any other."

"Hold it. Wait right there!" Grandpa George hurried back into his bedroom and quickly returned with a light blue beret and a long silk scarf.

"These belonged to your grandmother." Grandpa George carefully placed the hat on Louisa's head and looped the scarf around her neck.

"It goes like this," he said, tilting her hat a little to the side.

She twirled in front of the mirror. "Now I look like a real Parisian!"

Grandpa George smiled, although he looked as if he might cry. Louisa placed her hands under her grandfather's chin and kissed his cheek.

∞

On one side, Louisa clasped hands with her grandfather; on the other she clutched the handle of the tiny suitcase with her whole life packed inside. Neither she nor Grandpa George spoke as the train bound for Paris pulled into the station. Saying goodbye, she climbed the steps and waved to her grandfather through the window. With a jolt, the locomotive slowly pulled away.

Feeling homesick already, Louisa pulled her knees up to her chest and drifted off to sleep. Some time later, she awoke to the sound of the train's loud whistle. She rubbed her eyes and glanced at the man sitting next to her. His drooping jowls and shaggy moustache reminded her of Rosencrantz. He was even snoring softly, just as the dog did. He was also taking up half of her seat with his elbow, but she was too shy to tell him. Instead, she wedged herself further into the corner.

Louisa stared out the window until the purple silhouette of the Pyrenees Mountains faded into the distance and rectangular patches of green and mustard yellow fields replaced them. She listened dreamily to the sounds of the train car as it rocked rhythmically back and forth. Steadily, she detected a new sound like the tiny heartbeat of a mouse. She leaned towards the man, but the sound was not coming from his direction. Still, the ticking grew louder. It seemed to be coming from inside of her coat. She felt around the silk lining in her pocket until her fingers touched something smooth, cold and alive.

She lifted the pale gold mechanism from her pocket. On the face of it was a jumble of dials, hands, numbers and symbols that seemed to conform to some unearthly geometry. The hands on the various dials turned both clockwise and counterclockwise.

Louisa was gripped by the oddest feeling—the kind a person gets when they are being watched. She glanced around the cabin. The man next to her was still snoring, only now he inhaled with a laboured snort and exhaled with a long whistle. The unpleasant woman sitting across the aisle was busy shovelling crisps into her mouth by the handful. Behind her, an older gentleman was dozing off beneath his newspaper. Next to him, a teenaged boy was listening to his headphones and mouthing the lyrics into an imaginary microphone. *Yuck!* Louisa thought. *Teenaged boys are so ridiculous.*

But as usual, no one was paying any attention to her. Then slowly, a child's face peeked out from behind the seat, her bright eyes full of curiosity. Louisa was not too old to remember how children were often excellent observers, especially of the most secret things. Satisfied, she'd found her spy; Louisa turned her attention back to the mechanism. At first, she'd thought that it was some type of clock, but now she wasn't sure. Turning it over, she read the inscription etched into its case.

KEEP ME SAFE.

How odd. Louisa rested her index finger on one of the many jewelled buttons along the edge of the device. She pressed down and the hands stopped dead. Next, the timepiece clicked and the hands began to spin clockwise, faster and faster, until they were nothing but a blur.

Louisa released the button. There was a brief burst of light. The next thing that went through her mind was the incredibly distressing feeling of implosion.

Like a piece of popcorn being un-popped she began to shrink. First it was her fingers, then her arms. Finally, her body crinkled and collapsed. Her heart slowed and then stopped. She tried to scream, but some external force threw her voice right back down her throat. The sun was extinguished. The countryside vanished. The walls of the train, her seat, the floor, and the funny man sitting next to her, the awful woman eating crisps, the man dozing beneath his newspaper, the teenaged boy, the little girl—they all vanished. There was not a sound, not a vibration. There was no light or darkness. There was simply nothing. For an instant she was a speck floating in nothingness, a thought lost in a terrifying void.

Bit-by-bit, her body returned. Blood re-entered her veins; air inflated her lungs, and her heart once again thumped with life. She opened her eyes, feeling as if she had awoken from a fairytale sleep. The train was gone. The world was gone. The sight of what had replaced it shocked her.

Louisa remembered the feeling she'd had upon entering Old Trafford Football Stadium for the first time. She had been riding on her father's shoulders. Seeing such vastness had taken her breath away. What she saw before her now was indescribably more. Without intending to, she had found the gateway to a region that existed between the walls of time and space. She had stepped outside of the boundaries of her world into an endless abyss, a world beyond comprehension.

Louisa hung weightless in the centre of a cavernous tunnel that stretched out of sight in immense loops and curves. The walls were translucent and glowed faintly in colours she could not name. It seemed the hues did not fall within the range of anything known in the visible spectrum of light. Streaks of lightning crossed between the colossal passageways. Masses of prisms, clusters of cubes, bubbles and rapidly shifting polyhedral forms appeared and disappeared in time with the most baffling and tremendously loud noises.

She stared at her bizarre new surroundings, trying to find something—anything—familiar. It took her a few moments to realize she was moving. She was not climbing, flying, swimming, crawling or wriggling. No, instead, her movements were part voluntary and part involuntary. She was encased in a sphere, which became visible when it was struck by the surges of energy that pulsed along the tunnel. Louisa touched the surface of the bubble and a peculiar energy leapt from it. Startled, she pulled her hand away, but it was unharmed. Again, she waved her hand along the sphere's surface and once more the energy reached out to meet it.

Louisa glimpsed a tiny point of brilliant light streaking through a tunnel like a shooting star.

∞

If she'd had a closer look at the light, she would have seen that it was a sphere exactly like her own. If she'd been able to look inside of that sphere, she would have noticed an older gentleman with a kind, careworn face, casually standing as if he were waiting at a bus stop. Adalbert Uhrmacher was intently reading the news, although the news was rather old—four hundred and fifty-one years old, to be exact. At his feet was a worn leather briefcase and he was wearing a brown topcoat and matching Homburg hat, on top of which stood a large green parrot. Adalbert's eyes widened as he surveyed the vast netherworld spreading in every direction. No matter how many times he had journeyed into the wormhole, it never ceased to evoke in him a sense of wonder. The passageways always reminded him of the complex network of tunnels found beneath the cities of London, New York, Paris, and Tokyo. But while those could deliver a person *on* time, this could deliver a person *through* time.

How had Adalbert come to this lonely place? Was he on a secret mission of the highest importance? Was he attempting to unwind a paradoxical space-time conundrum that threatened the very existence of the universe itself? Not at that moment, no. The truth was, he was hurrying back home to turn off his stove. Adalbert had left the burner on. Just like Louisa, he was a time traveller, and he was doing what most time travellers do when they time travel: not very much.

It is true that time travellers can have extraordinary adventures, but this tends to be the exception and not the rule. For the most part, time travellers hardly ever have any adventures at all. But this is not entirely by choice. A wrong word uttered, a thought interrupted, an insect accidentally squashed—the tiniest alteration to the past might set in motion a chain reaction, unleashing a tidal wave of change, the results of which could be catastrophic.

For the most part, time travellers do things that other people would find quite mundane, like spying on their old dog for instance or attending their wedding—in a disguise of course. Often, Adalbert could be found crouching outside of his childhood home, waiting while his mother set a freshly baked apple pie on the windowsill, just to get a whiff.

His stomach did a summersault when the sphere

made a sudden drop and sped through a particularly tangled portion of the wormhole. While there were no forces of gravity inside Adalbert's fantastic craft, his mind never failed to trick his body into feeling as if there were.

The sphere plunged into a corkscrew-like tunnel and then entered a loop of gigantic proportions. As he approached the speed of light, Adalbert began to count. In free space, light travels just over one hundred and eighty-six thousand two hundred and eighty-two miles per second. Ten seconds passed as Adalbert entered the loop, traversed its length and then shot out the other side.

Adalbert checked his watch, an old habit that he'd never been able to kick—he was a time traveller after all. He folded his newspaper and tucked it up under his arm. The large parrot that had been sitting patiently on his head let out a "*Raaaaaaaaaaaaaaaarrrrrrrrrrrrp!*"

"What are we to do, Bruce?"

Under normal circumstances, he would be fretting about his upcoming exit from the wormhole and subsequent re-entry into the universe, a task that always made him nervous, no matter how many times he'd accomplished it. However, at that moment, there were far more troubling things on his mind.

∞

Louisa, of course, did not know any of this as she sped onwards into the void. Indeed, she was thinking that she ought to be getting back and wondered just how she might accomplish such a feat. And then, suddenly, she felt the strange sensation she'd felt earlier. Once again, her heart slowed and then stopped. She felt herself being stretched into a long, thin strand, like spaghetti. Again, there was no sound, no light and no darkness. There was nothing.

Louisa felt bones, muscles, veins and skin forming. She sensed herself filling out, rematerializing, as it were. Wincing, she rubbed her temples, afraid that her head might burst. Fortunately, the pain did not last. She breathed a sigh of relief when the terrible feeling subsided.

When she opened her eyes, she was standing on a bridge. The river sparkled with a million glittering reflections. The broad streets were lined with trees and elegant buildings. It was a clear, cool evening and the sky was turning from rose to violet. Louisa stood motionless, drinking in the lovely city. Somehow—beyond explanation—she was in Paris.

What just happened? Louisa reached for the timepiece and to her surprise she discovered something else in the pocket of her grandfather's coat. There was a letter with her name written on it in an elegant golden script. The envelope was sealed with rather important-looking red wax and stamped with a snake twisted into a figure eight.

SEPTEMBER 2nd, 2012

Pont Notre-Dame,

4th arrondissement,

Paris, France

CHAPTER THREE

The Dining and Social Club for Time Travellers

LOUISA CAREFULLY broke the seal of the mysterious letter. Inside she found an invitation.

Louisa Sparks,

You are cordially invited to join

The Dining

and

Social Club

for

Time Travellers.

Please accompany us

for an evening of fine dining at

8:15 p.m. punctually,

on

Sunday, September 2nd, 1717

At

Le Café Papillon.

Louisa scrunched her eyes closed. *I am having an odd dream. Soon I will wake up and be back on the train.* But the clock's incessant ticking filled the space around her. With each tick, her eyelids were pried back open until she stood, staring wide-eyed at the stubbornly real city.

Louisa read the letter again, but slower this time, concentrating on every detail. The name of the café stood out in her mind. She was sure that she'd heard of it. At first, she was not certain where or how, but gradually it came to her. The café was not far from the Seine River, where she was now. That summer she'd travelled to Paris with her grandfather and spent five glorious days exploring. They'd passed by the café on their final day. Grandpa George had pointed it out. It had been long abandoned, by the looks of it.

"The Dining and Social Club for Time Travellers—I've never heard of anything more ridiculous in my entire life!" Louisa studied the date. "September 2nd, seventeen-seventeen, I get it, someone is playing a trick on me."

But the ticking of the mysterious device grew steadily louder and to make matters worse, her stomach let out a loud *grrrrroooooooiiiinnnnnnk!*

"The invitation had said fine dining," she reasoned.

Don't you even think about it, young lady! Her mother's voice was clear in her mind.

Ab-so-lutely not! Her father's voice added.

Clearly, there was only one thing to do.

∞

The brick façade of the Café Papillon was crumbling, and the sign that hung over the window looked as if a gust of wind could blow it down. Louisa rubbed the windowpane with her sleeve, making a small circle in the thick layer of grime. She cupped her hands to the glass and surveyed the interior. A few bats fluttered around in the main dining room, and hundreds more hung upside down from the ceiling. The café was completely abandoned.

Louisa froze when she heard the shuffling of footsteps.

"Pleasant evening, is it not?"

She spun around, coming toe-to-toe with a frightful-looking man wearing tall black boots, a grease-stained overcoat and a wide-brimmed hat that hid most of his face.

"There is nothing quite like Paris at night. I especially like how the city lights reflect on the water." He spoke with a peculiar American accent as if he had stepped out of an old black and white movie.

Louisa stared at him, speechless.

"Oh drat!" the man exclaimed, checking his pockets in a very annoyed sort of way. "I know that I left it somewhere... Ah ha! Found it! No! Not it," he said, tossing a candy wrapper to the ground. "I thought that I had put it in my top-left pocket, but maybe it is in my bottom-right pocket, instead. Or, I know, maybe I left it in my—oh good! There it is!" He held up a jellybean between his thumb and forefinger. "Last one," he said, offering it to Louisa. "It's green, I think."

"No, thank you," Louisa chirped.

"Suit yourself." The man tipped his chin upwards and popped the jellybean into his mouth.

"Sir, it was nice chatting with you, but—" Louisa paused while she thought up an excuse. "You see, my parents are just around the corner waiting for me, and I really must be going or they will start to worry."

However, the man did not seem to hear her. "How did you do it?" he asked, chewing his jellybean.

Louisa knew she should go—but curiosity was taking over. "Do what?"

"The wormhole. How did you find it?"

"The wormhole?"

"Yeah, you know, the really big place with the giant tubes, loud noises, floating shapes and little balls of glowing white light zooming around? You were in the wormhole, were you not?"

"I guess I was," Louisa said timidly. "Or, at least, I think I was. But how did you know about that? I'm sure it was just a dream."

"I assure you it was no dream."

"Well, I suppose it couldn't have been a dream if you knew about it. Unless, I am also dreaming now."

"I'm as real as it gets, darlin'." He leaned forward, offering up his cheek to Louisa. "Go ahead, give it a pinch."

"I'll pass, thank you."

Undiscouraged, the man continued, "So?"

"So, what?"

"So, how did you do it? How did you find the wormhole?"

"Well, I guess I simply pressed a button."

"Simply pressed a button?" The man shook his head disapprovingly. "Lesson number one: never, under any circumstances, should you simply press a button."

Louisa took the device from her pocket.

"Your time machine, it's astonishing," he muttered under his breath.

"I'm sorry, did you say—"

"Time machine, yes," he snapped.

"Then, you must be a—"

"A time traveller?" he interrupted again. "Well, I suppose that I am. Mostly, I am just Edward Krunk. And you must be Louisa Sparks?"

"H-how do you know my name?" Louisa stammered.

"That is a very complicated question, one that I am not entirely sure how to answer. All I can say for sure is that you are on the list."

"The list?"

"Yes, that's correct. We have a guest list, and your name is on it."

"A guest list?"

"That's right."

"And my name is on it?"

"Indeed, it is."

"But how is that possible?"

"That too is an extraordinarily difficult question. And once again, it is one that I am not entirely sure how to answer. However, right now we must be going."

"Where to?" Louisa could not imagine that they would be dining inside of the café. There must have been a mistake on the invitation.

"The Café Papillon, of course!" Edward gestured towards the crumbling café. "I assume that you read the invitation, or you wouldn't be here."

"We're eating in there?" Louisa looked towards the café skeptically.

"That is correct."

"But it's disgusting."

"Actually, it's quite charming."

"Maybe there's another café close by?"

"Oh, we are definitely at the right place." A smile turned up the corners of Edward's mouth. "We're simply a little late." Just then, Edward's gaze shifted to something beyond Louisa and his smile sank. "Quickly, your time machine. Give it to me!"

But, Louisa refused to hand it over. "Why are you in such a hurry? If you really are a time traveller, you wouldn't be worried about being late."

"I would not try to steal the device if that is what you are insinuating. Although, there are others who would."

Still, Louisa refused to hand it over.

"There is no time to argue," Edward insisted. "We must hurry!"

Louisa followed Edward's gaze. Nearby, two shadowy figures observed them from inside of a sleek black car.

"There isn't a moment to spare!" Edward snapped. This time, Louisa passed the device to him. He quickly set to work turning the dials. "Now, take my hand."

As the tips of Louisa's fingers touched Edward's, she began to implode. *Oh, no,* she thought. *Not again.*

SEPTEMBER 2nd, 1717

The Café Papillon,

6th arrondissement,

Paris, France

When Louisa rematerialized, her temples throbbed with pain. Gritting her teeth and clutching the sides of her head, she did not dare open her eyes, afraid that her eyeballs might pop right out of their sockets.

"Hurts, doesn't it?" said a voice that sounded like Edward's, but she couldn't quite figure out where it was coming from. "Don't worry, it's just the crunch. Regrettably, there isn't anything you can do now but wait." Edward's voice sounded like a boot being pulled from the mud. "The crunch happens every time you time travel unless of course you eat a green jellybean. You see, jellybeans—particularly green ones—just happen to possess the exact chemical composition required to remedy the mind-scrambling effects of time travel. Absolutely nothing works better."

"*Urrrrrrrggggghhh!*" Louisa replied. Her headache was lessening but confusion was setting in. She gently rubbed her temples, trying to string together some logical thought. She'd believed that time travel was nothing more than science-fiction. And now, well...

Cautiously, Louisa opened an eye. What greeted it was a marvellous transformation. Gone were the broad thoroughfares lined with trees and elegant buildings. Instead, she saw a narrow, straw-covered laneway bordered by crooked black houses. An unhealthy air hung above them. This Paris was no longer the capital of luxury and taste; it was a dirty and dangerous looking place.

"Where are we?" she asked Edward, who appeared beside her from out of nowhere.

"Paris, of course."

Louisa tried a different approach. "All right then. *When* are we?"

"We are in the year seventeen-seventeen," Edward declared. "We have travelled nearly three centuries into the past."

"So, you mean to tell me that we time travelled here? That I—" She took a deep, trembling breath. "That I am a time traveller?"

"It would seem."

Louisa went to ask her next question *(How?)* but thought better of it. She knew what Edward's answer would be: *with extraordinary difficulty.*

Somewhere nearby, the clip-clop-clip-clop of horse hooves rang out and a lonely voice called: "Brooms for sale! Bellows or buckets to mend!"

The appearance of the Café Papillon had changed. The brickwork was neatly laid, and a freshly painted sign hung from its signpost. Puffs of smoke rose from a crooked chimney. The front door was open and a warm firelight flickered from within.

A man dressed in a yellow waistcoat trimmed with gold greeted Louisa and Edward at the entrance of the café. He wore matching yellow breeches with white socks pulled up to his knees and a splendid feathered hat with a wide brim turned up on three sides.

"Good eventide, my lady!" He bowed low, ceremoniously removing his hat. His long thin nose and domed forehead came level with Louisa's face. There was a vigorous intelligence in his heavy-lidded eyes. "Speak thy name, my lady!"

"My name is Louisa Sparks."

"Aye, methinks I know thy name. 'Tis most beauteous." The man plucked a pink rose from inside his waistcoat. As he lifted the flower, Louisa noticed his ring. It was engraved with the identical serpentine figure eight that had been stamped into the seal of the letter.

"Why, thank you." Louisa blushed. No one other than her mother had ever given her a flower. She held the lovely rose up and inhaled deeply.

"I am Rhadamanthus Finch." He bowed even lower this time. "Thy humble servant."

"What do you do exactly?" Louisa knew it was a silly question, but Rhadamanthus seemed delighted that she had asked.

"Why, my lady, I am a physicist, mathematician, inventor, philosopher, economist and alchemist, amongst many other things."

She pointed to Rhadamanthus' pinky finger. "The

symbol—on your ring—what does it mean?"

"'Tis the lemniscate, the secret sign of the time travellers." A curious expression crossed his face. "Has no one told you?"

She shook her head.

Rhadamanthus tut-tutted, then passed Louisa a cone-shaped wool cap with a pointed crown that curled forward. "I present to you the sacred coxcomb of the time travellers."

"Coxcomb?" she repeated.

"A hat, of course, my lady," Rhadamanthus chuckled and motioned for her to put it on her head.

She pulled the edges of the cap over her ears and turned to look for Edward, but he was nowhere in sight. The other time travellers were arriving in bursts of light and hurrying into the café. Each of them wore a purple hooded cloak that skimmed the ground. When the Club members passed Rhadamanthus, they winked and smacked their lips together noisily. *Another secret sign,* thought Louisa.

She could distinguish only one member from the rest, whose metal feet were clank, clank, clanking along the ground. As he noisily stepped past her, the two blank disks of his spectacles gleamed from underneath his hood, instilling in her a vaguely familiar feeling.

"Let us go hither," Rhadamanthus said, beckoning to

Louisa as he closed the heavy wooden door behind them and slid the bolt into place. The low-ceilinged chamber was lit only by firelight and was full of rare and finely crafted furnishings. Placed in the middle of each table was an enormous goblet piled high with green jellybeans.

Once safely inside and away from prying eyes, the time travellers removed their cloaks and adorned their conical shaped caps. Louisa counted twelve members in total—thirteen when she included herself. There was a podium set near the fireplace. On it rested a large, red leather-bound book.

A boisterous murmur circulated the room when she entered. Rhadamanthus ushered her to her seat. A boy, who couldn't have been much older than Louisa, sat next to her. He had a twitchy little nose and brown eyes that brimmed with mischief.

"My name is Gendun." He cocked an eye towards a bulging, warted woman with a bent back and long crooked nose. "That's Brünnhilde. She's a witch."

"A real witch?" Louisa whispered.

"Oh yes, dearie, I am 'ze genuine article," came Brünnhilde's croaking voice.

Louisa's eyes dropped and her hands busied themselves with the tablecloth.

"Not to vorry, dearie, I vould never cast a spell on a nice lee-tle girl such as yourself—but as for YOU—you thee-ving street urchin," she said, pointing a gnarled finger at Gendun, who shifted in his seat uncomfortably. "I vould turn you into a toad 'zis instant."

He took a quick look at the witch and her eyes flashed menacingly back at him.

"Are you a real thief?" Louisa asked.

A crisp, synthesized voice answered. "Gendun is a swindler and a pickpocket who works the train stations and busy marketplaces of France." Everything but the mechanical man's face was a flashing cluster of gears, wire and steel and he had two glowing telescopic lenses in place of eyes. "When Gendun is near, a temporarily distracted shopkeeper might discover that he has six loaves of bread instead of seven and twelve apples instead of thirteen—"

"I WAS a swindler and a pickpocket," Gendun interjected. "But, I've retired—at least temporarily—from stealing."

"Vonce a thief, alvays a thief," Brünnhilde warned.

The mechanical man held an accordion-like index finger in the air. "I am a firm believer that, ex-offenders should be afforded a second chance to become productive citizens."

Gendun haphazardly pointed his thumb at the mechanical man. "The tin man's name is Radicon Spring. He's a cybrid."

"Oh, I see." Still confused, Louisa asked, "What's a cybrid?"

"Cybrid's are part human and part machine." With a click and a whir, Radicon extended his snake-like arm across the table to greet her. "It is delightful to meet you."

Louisa couldn't help but laugh when she shook his hand.

"What's so funny?" Gendun asked.

"I was not expecting him to sound so, well—no offence to Mr. Radicon—so human," Louisa whispered to Gendun.

Radicon lit up all over, reminding Louisa of the Eiffel tower at night. "Why, thank you, young lady!"

A commotion arose from a corner of the room where three men were engaged in a heated debate regarding the shape of the earth. Two were vying for round, and one hulking figure was insisting that the world was flat. He hammered the table with his massive fist. A storm was brewing inside of the Viking's mysterious, deep-set eyes that were the colour of the coldest regions of the sea. The plump face of the friar had turned bright red, and the three men were shouting all at once.

"In case, you were wondering, that's Theoderic, Sigermus and Alpharabius." Gendun rolled his eyes at the trio. "Those bigmouths have been arguing about the same thing for months."

Another disturbance erupted at the rear of the café. Louisa turned to see Edward Krunk battling the arms of a scrawny but fierce woman craning her head inside the dining hall. Edward just about caught her nose in the door when he slammed it shut.

Gendun shook his head. "That's Ezmè, the innkeeper's wife. She's not supposed to be in here."

"Do the innkeeper and his wife know about the time travellers?"

Gendun inched closer to Louisa. "Of course not. They think they are hosting The Lemonade-Makers Guild. It is one of the many guises used by the Club."

"But that's a lie."

He lowered his voice. "Frequent deceptions are a regrettable but necessary part of ensuring the Club's safety. It is essential that our identities remain secret."

Looking very different without his disguise, Edward fixed his cap onto his head and hurried towards the podium. He looked like he had been handsome once, but his hair had thinned, his chin had filled out and he had a distracted and irritable look about him.

Gendun continued, "Edward has been elected acting president until Adalbert Uhrmacher returns. His appointment has greatly displeased more than a few members. Though, I suspect none more than Edward himself. I don't think he likes being in charge one bit."

Edward dithered around in his pockets until finally, with a look of triumph, he found his cue cards.

"Do you know Adalbert?" asked Louisa.

At that, Gendun puffed out his chest like a silly bird. "I don't like to brag, but I practically taught him everything he knows."

Brünnhilde let out an irritated, "*HUMPH!*"

"Well, he's more like a mentor," he said, sounding a little deflated. "Adalbert took me under his wing—made me his apprentice."

"Is 'zat 'vut you like to call svee-ping floors?" Brünnhilde croaked.

"At least, I don't *ride* a broom," Gendun retorted.

"At least, I dee-dn't have to hee-tch a ride. You see, Gendun is not a *real* time traveller, dearie."

"Oh, what do you know? You warty old toad!" Gendun looked instantly regretful. His skin had turned pale green and his tongue involuntarily poked out to taste the air.

Brünnhilde made a horrible cackle.

Edward shot the witch a disapproving glance and Gendun's complexion was restored.

"Order! Order!" Edward called, striking the podium repeatedly with his gavel. No one was listening. Conversations were in full swing around the room, and the din was rising higher and higher.

"Shush! Everyone-a, pleash stop-i-da talking!" An elderly Italian man was standing with his hands raised. His curling grey beard fell over his chest and his eyes were like two bright orbs. An immediate hush fell over the room.

"Is that... Leonardo da Vinci?" Louisa whispered, scarcely believing her eyes.

Gendun nodded.

"Thank you, Leo," Edward said.

Promptly, da Vinci sat down and went back to scribbling in his notebook, his quill moving rapidly over the pages from right to left.

"Now, gentlemen—"

Brünnhilde let out another irritated, "*HUMPH!*"

"And ladies," Edward added quickly. "We have many things to cover before we eat."

At the mention of food, Louisa's stomach grumbled. In her excitement, she'd forgotten how hungry she was.

"I will dispense with the pleasantries," Edward continued.

"Edward is always dispensing with the pleasantries," Gendun whispered, "Which is, in my opinion, one of the chief reasons why he's so unpopular. Adalbert always knew what to say and just when to say it—Edward has an extraordinary talent for just the opposite."

"First off, is everyone wearing their name tag?"

Edward pleaded and the time travellers groaned.

"In addition to being rather abrupt," Gendun chimed in again. "Edward is also a stickler for the rules, which, as you can tell, further contributes to his unpopularity."

"I know, I know!" Edward rolled his eyes. "Most of you need no introduction, but we have a new pledge with us this evening, so no exceptions."

"I deedn't get vone," came one worried voice.

"I hast lost mine," another whined.

"There is no cause for concern!" Edward held up a handful of nametags. "I have extras. And if anyone needs a quill to write with, there are plenty!"

Edward muttered some more rules to himself while he thumbed through the pages of the humongous red book.

"'Zat is 'ze official mee-nute book, dearie," croaked Brünnhilde. "It contains 'ze records of every meeting in 'ze Club's hee-story. It is customary at 'ze bee-gee-ning of each meal to read 'ze Club rules aloud," Brünnhilde continued.

Edward cleared his throat. "The objective of The Dining and Social Club for Time Travellers is for time travellers to dine together. The Club shall dine on alternate Sundays at 8:15 p.m., punctually." Edward looked around the room dramatically.

"He looovvees saying the next bit," Gendun chuckled.

Louisa was beginning to think that Gendun was a bit of a gossip.

Edward leaned over the podium. "The identities of the time travellers shall be wrapped in an impenetrable mystery!" A soft ahhh circulated amongst the members, who apparently liked hearing it just as much as Edward enjoyed saying it. "Next," he continued, "There is the matter of Louisa Sparks."

At the mention of her name, the time travellers turned to look at Louisa en masse, unleashing a host of butterflies inside her stomach. Louisa was feeling more than a little nervous at having been referred to as *a matter*.

"Esteemed time travellers," Edward began. "I ask that you consider electing Louisa Sparks as our newest member by gripping both earlobes and chanting the Club motto three times."

Louisa held her breath. Slowly, the members raised their hands to their earlobes and chanted, "Tempus neminem manet proximus!"

Brünnhilde slipped a green jellybean into the mouth of an enormous rodent poking its snout out from the folds of her clothing. "It means, time vaits for *almost* no-vone," she explained, but Louisa didn't hear her because she was staring at the huge rat. "Don't mind

Harold, dearie. Vhy, my rat, has more manners 'zan half of 'ze other time travellers." Brünnhilde scowled in the direction of two men who watched while the others cast their votes.

"That is Belthazzar and his greasy friend is Rogvolod," Gendun muttered.

Sitting still as two grim gargoyles, neither Belthazzar nor Rogvolod had tugged on their earlobes or uttered a single word.

What's their problem? Louisa wondered.

"It is settled," Edward declared. "We have reached a quorum. You have received a majority of votes and, therefore, have been elected to join The Dining and Social Club for Time Travellers," he proudly called out, "Louisa Sparks, please approach the podium."

With her knees wobbling, she hastened to the front of the room.

"Louisa Sparks, raise your right hand and make the secret sign of the time travellers. Just like this. Yes, that's it. No, no. Try again. Yes, that's right, you've got it. Now tuck your thumb in. No, no, like this, see? Good, good."

It took Louisa a few tries, but eventually she managed to get it right.

"Louisa Sparks, do you hereby solemnly swear to uphold the rules of The Dining and Social Club for Time Travellers?" Edward was holding a carefully folded purple cloak with a golden ring placed on top. Engraved on the ring was the symbol of the lemniscate.

"Yes," Louisa replied, as solemnly as she could.

"Then repeat after me..." Edward delved into a long, complicated list of rules and regulations, each of which she repeated—until he came to the final one.

"I shall *never*, under any circumstance, *alter the past*." Edward's eyes were locked on hers. A profound silence fell over the room.

Louisa had so many questions. *Could the past be altered? Could history be rewritten? Could I return to the night of their accident? Could I stop them from getting into the taxicab? Could I save my parents? Can I finally make my wish come true?*

"Louisa," Edwards's soft voice drew her back. "Each of us have had our disappointments, but we must never, under any circumstances, alter the past."

"I..." Louisa's voice was hesitant. The prospect of saving her parents lives had come and gone in a moment. Then, as if sensing her struggle, the members began to applaud, and her courage grew.

"I will never, under any circumstances... alter the past," she promised.

"Louisa Sparks, raise your left hand."

She raised her hand and Edward slipped the ring onto her pinky finger. Next, he unfolded the cloak and draped it over her shoulders. It was a perfect fit.

"Welcome, Louisa." A thundering applause erupted as the time travellers officially welcomed their newest member.

Not knowing what else to do, she scurried back to her seat, glad to be out of the spotlight.

"Next is the matter of dues," Edward said and another widespread groan circulated the room.

"He doesn't like to waste time, even though it annoys everyone to no end," Gendun snickered. "We are time travellers, after all."

Louisa gave Gendun a look—the same look she would have given a schoolmate who'd ratted out a friend for passing a note.

"But enough about Edward," Gendun said sheepishly. When he finally spoke again, he was smiling in an awkward sort of way. "Welcome to the Club, Louisa."

Louisa grinned back at her new friend, then turned her attention to Alpharabius, who had risen from his seat.

Alpharabius adjusted the long purple feather that jutted from his pumpkin-sized turban. He then unrolled a long piece of parchment and gave a short cough as he prepared to speak. "The members with outstanding fees are—"

He was abruptly cut off when the door of the elevator sprung open and released a plume of steam into the air. The dumbwaiter was loaded with plates of food and a pot of aromatic coffee. Enthusiastic chatter filled the room and Alpharabius slunk back to his seat, treasury business deferred. His lovely purple feather slumped over sadly. The first course had arrived just in time to save the pinchpennies.

∞

The innkeepers hands were as coarse and hard as a slab of limestone, and his son yelped as one of them caught him on the back of the head with a SMACK. The boy had dropped an entire pot of boiled potatoes onto the floor. The boy's name was Benedetto, although he'd become convinced from a young age that it was Noodlehead.

"Noodlehead!" the boy's father, Procopio, called after him. Benedetto scrambled to gather the potatoes with one hand and clutched the back of his head with the other. The lanky boy had to dodge his father's huge midriff as it swayed dangerously back and forth in the narrow kitchen lit only by the flames that leapt from the oven door. Several times he was nearly pinned to the wall, and more than once Procopio's cleaver grazed the top of his son's head.

Procopio and his wife, Ezmè, had signed a lengthy agreement that bound them to absolute secrecy. It was made clear that the members of The Lemonade-Makers Guild must dine in complete privacy. Even before the contract was finalized, a member of the Club had carefully inspected the premises to ensure that it was adequately private and, most importantly, soundproof. If the café was found to be lacking on this latter point, alterations would have to be made. "It is no use dining in privacy if conversations can be overheard through a vent or an opening in a wall," the Club inspector insisted.

The food was to be prepared in the kitchen located below the dining room by Procopio and Ezmè. No one else was permitted to work in the café while the meeting was being held, and under no circumstances could any contact be made with a Club member. The meal was to be delivered to the dining room by a hand-operated elevator that moved between floors, and would be served by one of the Guild members. But Ezmè—a nosy and suspicious woman—had a way of disappearing when there was work to be done, so Procopio had smuggled his son into the kitchen to act as his sous-chef.

"Noodlehead! Go-a find-a your mama and make-a sure she's not-ta causing any-a trouble." Procopio shook his fist at Benedetto, who scurried away to find his mother while the time travellers' dinner was sent up the elevator shaft.

The main course was a carefully guarded recipe: lamprey eel was a delicacy reserved for kings and queens. That night Procopio had prepared it, especially, for his esteemed guests. He had cut the eel's head off and let the blood drip into a jar filled with vinegar. After peeling away the skin, he stewed the meat with shallots, leeks and pork fat. He finished the dish by pouring the clotted blood over it for the sauce. The Guild had paid Procopio handsomely for his particular attention and utmost discretion, and he was not about to disappoint.

Elsewhere, through a carefully concealed hole in the wall—an opening that even the Club's inspector had missed—an eye flicked back and forth, taking in the eccentric gathering. If poor Benedetto were searching for his mother, he needn't have looked any further...

∞

Upstairs, the limbs of a decrepit suit of armour jerked and clouds of dust shot forth from its stiffened joints. The suit shifted and emitted a loud screech. Its hollow boots clanged against the floor as it rigidly marched across the room to retrieve the entrée.

"What's that thing?" Louisa asked Gendun.

"The automaton is da Vinci's creation."

"The automa-what?"

"It's a robot, silly; da Vinci built it so that the Club members could dine in absolute privacy."

"Unfortunately, the absence of a live waiter does not always ensure complete freedom from nosy onlookers," Radicon interjected.

"Do you think someone could be spying on us?"

"Not a chance. I inspected the place myself," Gendun assured her.

A rather portly old friar waddled towards the front of the room, massaging his full stomach. The rest of the Club members hungrily lapped up the blood sauce and lamprey eel while Louisa filled up on the green jellybeans. Remembering the effects of the crunch, she snuck a few extras into her pocket for later.

"Sigermus is the Club's minute taker," Gendun explained. "He's also a little shy and a bit of a stutterer, but everyone likes him just the same."

Sigermus had a kindly face with big round eyes that had a funny way of blinking independently of one another. His thick-lensed spectacles perched on the end of his long nose accentuated this odd habit. The room quieted down, and every member of the Club leaned forward in anticipation. Standing on the tips of his toes, Sigermus prepared to give his address. He wetted his thumb with the tip of his tongue and searched through the pages of the thick minute book.

"There seems to be a bit of a p-p-problem," Sigermus stammered. "Things have changed somewhat. The last entry is *not* how I remember it."

"Sigermus suffers from delusions." A perfect look of displeasure was on the curve of Belthazzar's lips. "It is time that the idle-headed abbot retired."

Brünnhilde shot Belthazzar a nasty look. "He's not 'ze perfect gentleman 'zat he pretended to be 'ven he first joined 'ze Club."

"Fie! Let Sigermus speak." Theoderic folded his mighty arms across his massive chest.

Belthazzar's eyes flicked upwards. Louisa drew a quick breath at the sight of his star-shaped irises.

"He has 'ze eyes of 'ze devil," Brünnhilde said in a hoarse whisper.

"Sigermus has fallen out of his round tower and bumped his head." As he spoke, Belthazzar pinched a bit of dust from the sleeve of his immaculate coat.

Theoderic pounded the table, causing the jellybeans to jump. "Yea, continue, Sigermus. Pay no attention to that ill-mannered flap-dragon."

Crimson blotches had appeared everywhere on Sigermus' face, and his head had sunk into the collar of his shirt, like a nervous tortoise retreating into its shell.

"Speak on, Sigermus," Rhadamanthus urged.

Sigermus peered around the side of the podium at

Belthazzar and then timidly began once more. "There is no way to p-p-prove anything—you see, the p-p-proof exists only in my memory—but I am sure that the last entry has changed." Clucking his tongue disapprovingly, Sigermus flipped through the pages of the huge book, leaving the other members of the Club in suspense for some time. "It seems that other entries have b-b-been altered as well. Things that once were are no longer. The p-p-past, the p-p-present and maybe even the d-d-distant future have been d-d-distorted. Something has happened to cause a shift in the space-time c-c-continuum."

Belthazzar clapped his hands, diverting the attention of the time travellers. "Sigermus has eaten too much eel. The blubbering halfwit must have dozed off during dinner and had an unpleasant dream. This type of thing often happens to men who reach such great ages. Surely nothing's truly amiss?"

His voice carried a hypnotic rhythm that Louisa found unexpectedly calming. She looked around at the other time travellers, who seemed equally soothed by his words.

"Why, Belthazzar, do you so hastily dismiss his claims?" Once more, Theoderic broke his silence—and Belthazzar's spell.

Belthazzar turned on Theoderic. "I wonder, why are you so quick to agree with him?"

"Sigermus has always spoken the truth." Radicon's electronic eyes flashed to life.

There was a dangerous tremor in Belthazzar's voice. "Sigermus is a jabbering fool."

"And what of Adalbert?" Theoderic bellowed. "Where has he gone?"

"What of him?" A wicked grin teased the corners of Belthazzar's mouth. "The sentimental buffoon is probably hiding outside of his mother's house smelling the apple pies she sets out on the windowsill." Some of the other time travellers chuckled at this, though Louisa did not know why.

"Adalbert would not have left without warning," Radicon insisted, cutting off the smattering of laughter.

"How can you be sure that your beloved Adalbert hasn't abandoned you? It would not be the first time he'd done such a thing; I assure you. Or, perhaps he's had an accident?" Belthazzar glowered at the mechanical man.

"It vas no accident." Brünnhilde stood up to be heard. "Adalbert has been keed-napped!"

This allegation set off a flurry of outbursts. Sigermus' concerns had unleashed a flood of pent-up worry and frustration. It seemed as if many of the time travellers had been thinking the same thing.

"Kidnapped? Who would want him?" Belthazzar called out with a laugh.

"Adalbert has been taken by 'ze Nephilim," Brünnhilde croaked.

"Preposterous." Rogvolod's horrid voice escaped through the strands of greasy hair that hung across his face.

"I have foreseen it," Brünnhilde insisted.

"Lies," Rogvolod hissed, revealing his black gums and rotting teeth. "The Nephilim have not been seen in this world for two millennia." As Rogvolod spoke, his hands twitched, and his feet jerked beneath his coarse robe.

"Aye, an evil wind blows!" Theoderic pounded the table. "It will not be long before the tempest is upon us."

"There is no evidence that the Nephilim have returned!" Belthazzar roared.

"Do you, sir, call me a liar?" Theoderic pointed a finger at Belthazzar.

The room erupted in fiery debate and Louisa sank in her seat.

"It is true." The deep, gargling voice had an icy effect on the room and the time travellers fell silent.

Gendun whispered into Louisa's ear, "Amog lives in a place that cannot be reached, even if you travelled through space forever. He is from another dimension that is not part of this world."

The mysterious Amog remained motionless, except for the occasional flick of his blue forked tongue. His table was set apart in a shadowy corner, and he had not removed his hood or his black gloves. Though his heavy boots did not quite touch the ground, his broad shoulders and muscular frame were visible beneath his cloak. "The ranks of the Nephilim increase. The foul creatures walk amongst us once more. Sigermus is not mistaken. The space-time continuum has been disrupted. No war has been declared, but make no mistake, we are under attack."

Before anyone could utter another word, there was a *THUMP!* The front door of the café burst open and a swarm of policemen charged into the dining room armed with muskets, clubs, swords and daggers. In the lead was a triumphant Ezmè wielding a broomstick. "Witches! Warlocks! Devils!" she shrieked.

"No! No! No! Woman, what-a have-a you done?" came the innkeeper, Procopio's exasperated voice as he rushed in behind them. He had his hands on his head, and an expression of utter dismay was on his face. "We have-a not-a even served-a de gelato!"

Louisa watched in awe as, one by one, the time travellers vanished. Before she knew it, everyone had disappeared—except for her and Radicon. She was in such a panic that she could only stare open-mouthed at the angry lynch mob advancing upon her.

Louisa felt the heat from the fireplace at her back as

the pack of policemen closed in. She was preparing to raise her hands and surrender when Radicon snatched the fireplace poker and used it to knock the embers out of the hearth. Hot ash swirled up into the air, leaving Ezmè and her henchmen stumbling blindly inside a cloud of thick smoke. Louisa felt the weight of a hand on her shoulder.

"Time to go," came Radicon's crisp, synthesized voice.

Before the dust settled, Louisa and Radicon had escaped—up the crooked chimney on a rope ladder that had suddenly dropped down inside of it. They emerged from the mouth of the smokestack covered in soot.

"Well, it seems we have landed on our feet," Radicon said, brushing off his cloak.

"Nay, danger is still at hand." Rhadamanthus pointed to the street.

Ezmè's shrill voice could be heard screeching orders as she burst from the door of the café, followed by a parade of police. "'Ze roof! 'Ze roof!" she howled.

"Yarely! There is no time to spare. Into the time machine!" Rhadamanthus bounded into a craft that was fashioned from a type of large sled. The inside of the time machine was a confusion of levers, pedals, dials, glowing crystals, flashing lights and tangled wire.

Louisa hurried after Radicon into the cockpit of

Rhadamanthus' time machine. An explosion sounded as the policemen discharged their muskets, sending a volley of iron balls flying over their heads. Rhadamanthus snorted as one blew a hole clean through the top of his hat.

Louisa peered over the edge while Rhadamanthus frantically worked the foot pedals and levers inside of the disorderly cabin. Snooping townspeople wandered into the street to watch the policemen who had gathered in a semi-circle around the café. "Ready," the police captain cried. "Aim!"

Inside of the time machine, crystal shards lit up in an array of colours. The craft began to vibrate and hum. Louisa braced herself as the sled started to rise.

"*FIRE!*" the captain cried. Another explosion of muskets sounded, and a volley of iron balls passed through the air where the craft had just been.

The three time travellers clung to whatever they could while the sled bounced into the wormhole, like a pinball. Sparks flashed as the craft tipped dangerously from side to side.

Rhadamanthus' hands raced over the console in a mad attempt to bring the time machine under control. Just as Louisa thought that they would be dashed to pieces, the sled evened out when it entered into a long, straight passage. For a long while the three travelled through the infinite corridors of the wormhole in silence.

Louisa had many questions, but it took some time for her to muster up enough courage to speak. "What happened to Adalbert?" she finally asked.

"No one knows for sure, but some of us—as you heard—suspect he was kidnapped," said Radicon.

"By the Nephilim?"

"So it would seem," Radicon answered.

"Who are the Nephilim?"

Rhadamanthus spoke in a grave tone. "Those cursed half-men, those fallen angels. They are what lurks in thy worst nightmares. They are dread and insecurity. They are the black things that rise from underneath the beds of children at night, tall and thin with eyes that glow red and fingers like scythes. They have been called by many names: Gulyabani, Baba Yaga, Oude Rode Ogen, Namahage, Croque-mitaine, Old Bloody Bones, and a thousand more. Alas, their ancient and true name is Nephilim. They are from the oldest and greatest of Earth's cities."

Louisa tried to recall the oldest cities that she'd ever heard of. "Do you mean to say that the Nephilim are from Constantinople or Athens? Or, perhaps from Babylon?"

"There are places far more ancient than those, my lady."

"Like Atlantis?" It was a better guess than she'd intended.

"Precisely!" Radicon exclaimed.

"But, I thought that Atlantis wasn't real, that it was just a myth."

"Oft' what one thinks is not what truly is. I say, my lady, 'tis fact. In a single day and night of misfortune, the island of Atlantis disappeared into the depths of the sea." Rhadamanthus chanted in a very slow and somber tone: "Omnia mutantur, nihil interit."

Louisa moved closer to Radicon. "That last bit, what did he mean by it?" She was far too shy to ask Rhadamanthus, who seemed so lofty and wise.

"It is a very old saying, difficult to translate exactly, but what I think Rhadamanthus meant was that all things change, but nothing is ever destroyed."

"Aye," said Rhadamanthus. "Now, where can we drop you off, my lady?"

Louisa explained what train she had been on, the location of her seat, and the exact time that she had accidentally left it.

"Tricky, tricky," Radicon said, rubbing his chin.

"Is there a problem?" Louisa asked timidly.

Radicon's telescopic eyes zeroed in on Louisa. "Leaving the universe is problematic, but getting back to it, or, at least, getting back to the same place that you left off, is infinitely harder. Imagine a train travelling at an average speed of fifty-nine miles per hour. At the same time, it's also rising and falling and moving from side to side. Now picture the planet as it turns on its axis at a thousand miles per hour while simultaneously circling the sun at sixty-seven thousand miles per hour. Now envision the entire solar system as it travels through the universe at five hundred and fifteen thousand miles per hour. Finally, try to think of a way to get back on the train without rematerializing somewhere, on top of it, underneath it–or worse–half way in and half way out of it."

By the time Radicon had finished speaking Louisa was looking extremely pale. "Couldn't you just drop me off in Paris?"

"Nay, my lady. You must return to the precise moment you left or risk causing a rift in the space-time continuum," Rhadamanthus cautioned. "Alas, time travelling is a complicated business; in fact, on occasion, it can be downright dangerous. There are, after all, a number of things that can go wrong."

Louisa had no time to protest before she felt the tingle of dematerialization beginning in her toes. Bit-by-bit her surroundings dropped away until the only thing that remained were Radicon's gleaming telescopic eyes. "Radicon? Rhadamanthus?" But, there was no sign of the time travellers.

Louisa had the impression of swimming up into the train from an underwater world. The sun, the countryside, the man sitting next to her, the woman eating crisps, the man dozing beneath his newspaper, the teenaged boy and the little girl had reappeared. At first, she was convinced that she'd had a peculiar dream until she noticed the flash of the golden ring on her pinky finger.

SEPTEMBER 2nd, 2012

Gare du Nord,

10th arrondissement,

Paris, France

CHAPTER FOUR

Belthazzar's Lair

GRANDPA GEORGE had arranged for Louisa to stay with his distant cousin, Hignard, while she was attending school in Paris. Hignard, a lifelong bachelor, lived in a large red brick house, in the 4th arrondissement, with only his housemaid, his butler and an old Wolfhound named Rolf for company. She dreaded the thought of living with him. His house sounded so lonely and from the description she'd received, she imagined he would not be very friendly.

As Hignard had promised, he was waiting for her outside of the train station, sitting straight-backed, reading his newspaper in the back seat of his Rolls Royce. The boot was open in anticipation of her luggage. His butler was standing along side of the car holding a sign with Louisa's name on it.

Just like Grandpa George, Hignard was from England, although he had followed solitude and not love across the English Channel. He much preferred comfortable chairs and the latest periodicals to people. In Paris, everyone was far too self-important to pay any attention to him, and that was the way he preferred it.

The relationship between Hignard, Grandpa George and Louisa was difficult to trace. Grandpa George had tried several times to explain, but she could never quite get it straight. "You see, Louisa, it's really very simple. Your great, great grandmother, Arabella, married a man named Albert Honeycutt, and they had nine children; their seventh child, Neville, twice remarried. Neville's third wife, Lady Wincrest Gay, had four children, the youngest of which was Hignard. That makes Hignard your second cousin twice removed, why, I am almost sure of it."

In the end, Louisa and Grandpa George agreed that she would refer to her soon-to-be guardian as Uncle Hignard.

"Mademoiselle Sparks?" The salamander-like butler greeted Louisa with a miserable grin. His tuxedo hung shapelessly from his bony shoulders, and his eyes were like two black buttons.

When she was seated in the car, Hignard neatly folded his newspaper, leaned forward and trained his eyes on her. He had a severe look on his face, and the unlit pipe clenched between his teeth hovered dangerously close to her nose, but his scowl unexpectedly turned into a smile. "Hignard Randolph Aloysius Honeycutt, at your service."

Uncle Hignard removed his cap and smoothed the wisps of silver hair on his balding, but well-shaped, head. His hat, vest, suit and bow tie were various colour combinations of plaid, and he had an enormous crimson peony pinned to the lapel of his jacket. "Well, don't just sit there looking like an envelope without an address on it. Say something," Hignard yapped.

"Um," Louisa replied, feeling horribly shy. But it did not matter; Hignard had already started reading again.

"It was not easy, you know," he announced from behind his newspaper.

"Pardon me?" she asked.

"Why, I'm referring to the newspaper, you foolish girl. It was with no small degree of difficulty that I arranged for *The London Royal Times* to be delivered to my door every morning. The French do not take kindly to people enjoying things that are not from France, especially when those things happen to be from England."

Louisa did not take kindly to being called foolish, but she couldn't bring herself to say anything.

Hignard tilted his chin upwards as if they were about to start moving. Nothing happened. "Planchet! What in the world are you doing, man?" he called out the window to the butler, who was beetling around the outside of the car. "We shall all be dead from extreme old age before you finally get around to driving us home."

Planchet leapt into the driver's seat, and the engine rumbled to life.

"Finally, off we go," Hignard muttered. "Why, it's nothing short of a miracle." With a jolt, the car merged into the rush of traffic along the busy street. "Can you believe what they are passing off as news today? It says right here," he was stabbing at the paper with his finger, "That pterodactyls were seen nesting on the Tower Bridge, and that a massive prehistoric bird was spotted flying around Paris. Paris of all places! They are calling it a Giant Archaeopteryx. What rubbish."

"An Archaeopter-which?" Louisa asked.

But Hignard wasn't listening.

"What's the holdup, Planchet?" Hignard thumped

the roof with his umbrella. "I say, do you need me to drive the blasted car?"

The Rolls Royce was stopped behind a delivery van that was blocking the entire Rue Saint-Honoré. Behind them, traffic was backed up down the street. People were honking their horns and shouting at the unconcerned deliveryman who was casually unloading dresses from the back of his van.

"Overtake! Overtake!" Hignard ordered. "Use the sidewalk if you must."

The engine of the Rolls Royce roared, and they drove up onto the sidewalk. An armload of dresses went flying into the air as the deliveryman dove out of the way.

"You guinea pig!" the man shouted while he scrambled to recover the dresses.

"Good day to you, sir." Hignard waved his hat out the window as they drove off.

Louisa wanted to say, *Uncle Hignard, you could get into a whole lot of trouble doing a crazy thing like that.* Instead, she just watched the colourful fabrics float to the ground.

The Rolls Royce raced towards the Arc de Triomphe and entered into a massive eight-lane roundabout swarming with vehicles. Louisa wondered how everyone didn't just crash into one another. A police officer stood amongst the sea of cars. His white gloves were moving with lightning speed, and the shrill sound of his whistle rang out while he directed the traffic. A woman deftly navigated her bicycle through the busy roundabout, her lovely yellow coat and long white scarf catching the breeze behind her.

As they exited the roundabout, Louisa caught a glimpse of something very unusual indeed. Perched atop the Arc de Triomphe was a monstrous black bird, much bigger even than an ostrich. It had feathered wings that resembled an eagle's, the jagged teeth of a crocodile, the long, spiky tail of a lizard and the hideous head of a vulture. Crumbling stone dropped from where its razor-sharp talons cut into the monument's edge. Her eyes widened into two perfect circles. "Uncle Hignard, look it's the Archaeopteryx!"

Hignard just unfolded a pair of reading glasses, perched them on the end of his nose and then hid once again behind his newspaper. Louisa blinked in disbelief, wondering if there was any use in trying to speak to him at all. And the butler—who had evidently stopped listening to anything unless it began with the shouting of his name—did not hear her either.

The Archaeopteryx spread its vast wings and with one mighty sweep; the great bird took to the air.

SEPTEMBER 2nd, 2012

The Catacombs,

14th arrondissement,

Paris, France

Covering his nose with a silk handkerchief, Belthazzar entered the passage that led into the abandoned train station. Grotesque faces leered at him from the shadows. He returned their gaze with only a grim fascination. To him, they were nothing but dust. Striding ahead, without the aid of a light, he went—by a secret passage—into the closed-off gypsum mines. Darkness meant nothing to Belthazzar, who had grown so accustomed to the underground that he could see in the night better than in the light of day. He passed through the damp mineshaft and then into the sprawling necropolis where human bones were stacked ten feet high and ten feet thick along the corridors, under the district of Montparnasse. When he entered the ancient catacombs, a frigid puff of air drifted up from its recesses to greet him.

Standing very close to the wall, he ran his fingers over the skulls. He found an edge and moved sideways through a hidden opening. Water bled from fissures in the chalky walls and trickled along the milky floor of the narrow pathway. He travelled gradually downwards until he reached the base of a spiral staircase hewn from the living stone and then climbed the uneven steps.

He emerged from the narrow stairway into a cavern of reddish brick. At the opposite end, water trickled out of a hoary crevice into a reservoir that encircled the base of what looked to have been a massive fortification. An ancient stone bridge stretched across the moat towards an iron gate, barring the entrance to an underground castle.

"Gatekeeper! Open the gate." Belthazzar crossed the bridge and upon his approach, a weighty chain shifted, and the iron-latticed gate began to rise. The guard wore a coarse robe with a hood that disguised his face. When Belthazzar passed through the archway, the guard raised a clawed hand in salute.

∞

In a lightless cell no larger than four paces in each direction, a man lay on the cold hard floor without a single comfort, not a bed or even a stool to sit on. He stirred at the sound of footsteps.

"Who is there? Where am I? Rascals! I demand that you set me free!"

The man shielded his eyes from the dim light that filtered in suddenly through the slat in the doorway.

"I trust you are finding the accommodations to your liking? There are but a privileged few who know of the dungeons hidden below the streets of Montparnasse."

"I'm glad you find this amusing," the prisoner huffed. "Well, I assure you that I do not, and neither will the police."

"Even if you could escape, you and I both know that you would never go to the police. That would be far too risky for a man over four centuries old. Wouldn't you agree—time traveller?"

"What do you want from me?"

"It is a simple thing really, Adalbert—my old friend."

"Belthazzar? What is the meaning of this?"

There was the sound of a key entering a lock. The hinges of the cell door moaned when it was pushed open. A sack was pulled over Adalbert's head, and he was made to walk for a long while, down and down, until his legs had barely any strength left in them. He gasped when the sack was pulled from his head. He was stretched across a table and shackles were clapped onto his wrists and ankles. Adalbert stared fearfully at the tube that had been inserted into his arm.

"The intravenous contains a crystalloid solution that will deliver nutrients directly into your blood. I wouldn't want you complaining that I hadn't fed you." Belthazzar snatched the handkerchief out of Adalbert's breast pocket and dabbed the perspiration from his prisoner's forehead. "It also contains a truth serum."

"Get your filthy hands off me!" Adalbert struggled to free himself, but it was no use.

"I have become an expert at judging a man's nature. And I think that I can tell just what kind of man you are, Adalbert. You see, you have a particular stink; all your type does." Belthazzar viciously grabbed a hold of Adalbert's nose. "It smells like the long and comfortable life of a coward."

"Pray, there is no need to start insulting people." Adalbert's voice sounded pinched. "Why, it's hardly fair calling someone a coward while they are tied up and defenseless."

"I assure you, praying won't do you any good here, Adalbert."

"Upon my word, I will not stand for this treatment! I say, there are laws! Do you hear me? Laws!"

"Laws? Laws were created for milk-livered toadstools like you, not great men like me."

"Why, I have never heard such nonsense in my entire life."

"Tell me, Adalbert, have you ever witnessed a man being stretched on the rack? When his joints pop out of place, they make the funniest noise. Pop! Pop! Pop!" Belthazzar sang. "But that is just the beginning. When the tendons finally break, there is the most alarming snap!"

"Good heavens, I should say I have not! What an unspeakable thing to ask."

There was a tick, tick, tick as the chains fastened to Adalbert's wrists and ankles strained.

"No, you mustn't. You really mustn't!" Adalbert was

slowly being lifted off the table. He howled as the chains wrenched even tighter. "By gum, you will pull my arms right out of their sockets!"

"That would be a kindness in comparison to what I have in store for you."

"What have I ever done to you? I don't deserve this! Help! Someone, help me!"

"Silence!" Belthazzar shrieked, "If you listen carefully and do what I say, I might be persuaded to let you go."

"I'll tell you what you can do—you can go and get stuffed. I will never cooperate."

"Oh, I expect that you will, everyone does in the end." The tips of Belthazzar's fingers came to rest on an ornate box, set on top of a pedestal. On its face were five concentric rings of various sizes, inscribed with numbers and astrological symbols. The hands of the multiple dials rotated both clockwise and counterclockwise.

Belthazzar's hand glided over the surface of the mechanism. "I have acquired many things over the centuries, but not since the age of Atlantis, have I found anything like this. The mechanism's singular design and faultless artistry are nearly unequalled. But, I happen to know that another time machine was built, one so powerful that its maker hid it away in a place where no one could ever find it. Except for me of course, because you were just about to tell me where it is."

Adalbert's features hardened and he pulled against his restraints.

"Do not tire yourself uselessly, old friend. The chains are crafted from Atlantean steel, the hardest substance in the universe."

"Scoundrel!" he howled. "Thief!"

Undaunted, Belthazzar continued, "I realized long ago that there are only a few types of people in this world, and every one of them so tiresomely predictable. Still, there are elements about them that remain stubbornly elusive. My machines have a way of bringing out a person's true nature. For instance, how far can a man be pushed, before he betrays his most cherished friend, or reveals his most guarded secret? For some, it takes only a nudge, and for others—well, let's just say that's when it gets interesting." Belthazzar drew close to Adalbert so that the tips of their noses nearly touched. "Now, tell me, where have you hidden your precious time machine?"

"Villain, you are meddling with forces beyond your control."

Belthazzar casually inspected the glittering chains. "Atlantean steel, as you know, contains other unique properties that make it ideally suited for the distortion of time. The chains fastened to your wrists and ankles, when energized, will form a gravitational well. For each minute that passes outside of the well, a year will go by inside of it. In a minute from now, by my watch that is, you will have spent one agonizing year lying motionless on this table. In two minutes, you will have aged two years. In three minutes, I imagine that you will have completely lost your mind. I like to call it *divine intervention*."

"Blast it all, you won't get away with this!"

"But, don't you see? I already have." Belthazzar laughed wickedly.

Adalbert seemed to exhale a thousand breaths, and his hair and fingernails began to curl. His beard sprouted past his hollowing stomach, his hair thinned and turned white and he felt suddenly stricken, shrunken and old. "What is happening to me?"

"Where is the time machine, the one you call the Parallax?"

"I don't know," Adalbert gasped.

"Liar!" Belthazzar shook with rage. "Tell me, before it is too late, where is the Parallax?"

Adalbert's reply was barely audible. "The Parallax is lost."

∞

Without pause, Belthazzar strode up and up the spiral staircase into the clock tower. The clock's gears slowly turned around him as he surveyed its inner workings. A massive black bird folded his wings when he came to rest along the edge of a precipice jutting out from the clock tower. A man with skin as pale as salt, clapped an iron ring around the beast's ankle. The Archaeopteryx tugged at the heavy chain.

"What wonders have lived and died in this world, Rogvolod?"

The monk bowed low as Belthazzar stood before him, tall, cruel and kingly. "Many wonders, Belthazzar." His hands twitched, and his feet jerked nervously beneath his robe.

"Yet, why is it that some persevere while others vanish forever?" Belthazzar studied the Archaeopteryx with intense interest. "What caused this majestic species, this perfect killing machine, to vanish from the world over two hundred million years ago?"

Rogvolod raised a strip of shivering meat, and the hideous vulture's head drooped down low on its crooked neck. The monk tossed the meat in the air, and the bird gulped it down hungrily. The Archaeopteryx's cry echoed over the rooftops of the city.

"Patience, Golyath. The time will come when you can once again take to the skies freely." The Archaeopteryx staggered back and spread his wings menacingly when a bloated spider crept up onto Rogvolod's shoulder. "Atropos, my beauty." He lifted his hand to the arachnid's dreadful mouth and she sunk her fangs into his wrist. Black blood trickled down his colourless arm.

"Tell me, Rogvolod, what news do you bring?"

The monk stroked the coarse hairs along the arachnid's spiny back. "The trap is set. One by one, the little flies wander into our web." With pinching steps, the spider crawled down Rogvolod's body and squeezed her bulbous abdomen through a gap in the floor. "Soon, the time travellers will be erased and then, Belthazzar, you alone will possess the power to travel through time."

"Well done, Rogvolod. Still, an even greater web must be spun, an intricate one, the strands of which will stretch from the very dawn of civilization until the end of time."

A colossal pendulum swung inside the clock, and the gears began to turn, gradually, at first, and then faster and faster until they were nothing but a blur. Springs, levers and jewelled wheels spiralled as the cosmic engine whirred to loud life. "From its centre, I will hold the very fate of the world in my grasp. The great play will have a new author. Piece by piece the past will be altered." The inner workings of the clock changed into a celestial atlas with Belthazzar and Rogvolod standing at its centre. A tremor shook the entire structure. "There will be a new world order, and all earth's kingdoms will pay homage to me, and it will be as if it always was." Belthazzar's voice became distorted as he dematerialized. "For he who controls the past will rule the future!"

SEPTEMBER 2nd, 2012

Hignard's House,

4th arrondissement,

Paris, France

CHAPTER FIVE

A Collection of Oddities

"WELCOME HOME," Hignard announced when the car pulled to a stop.

Louisa opened the door and stared up at the magnificent red brick house. It was not like her crumbly old home in England or Grandpa George's tiny country cottage. Hignard's stately mansion faced a courtyard lined with tall linden trees clipped into perfect rectangles. A light breeze sent shadows from their branches dancing across the manicured lawn.

"Do stop dawdling, Planchet," Hignard cried with a stamp of his umbrella. "You know I can't stand it when you dawdle."

Planchet stood by the car's boot, fumbling with the keys.

"Go on and take Louisa's bags up to her room. And for Pete's sake man, get a move on. I say, you must be related to a snail."

She'd had just about enough. "You know Uncle Hignard, you really shouldn't speak to Planchet that way. You might hurt his feelings."

"Feelings? Poppycock. Planchet doesn't have any feelings. He hardly has a brain in his tiny head. Moreover, that halfwit is practically stone-deaf. He wouldn't know what I was saying if I climbed down his ear canal and kicked the Morse Code out on his eardrum."

After Hignard's impetuous speech, Louisa went straight upstairs to find her room. She feared she'd be counting the days until she returned to her grandfather's house.

Upon entering her new bedroom, she shivered. It felt far too large and drafty. The furniture was worn, and a thick layer of dust clung to every surface. Clearly no one had set foot inside for quite some time. Though, to her surprise, she noticed a very pleasant little balcony with fancy iron railings. She pulled open the door, which stuck a bit, as those old doors tend to do, and stepped outside.

Looking out over the rooftops, Louisa took a deep breath. There was a pleasant scent in the air, and the sky was streaked with pink. In the distance, the iron lattice of the Eiffel Tower gleamed in the early evening light. The grand old bridges reached across the sparkling water of the Seine like an enormous ribcage connecting the Left Bank to the Right Bank. To the north, the majestic domes of the Sacré-Cœur rose up high on the hilltop. The setting sun coloured the buildings of Paris gold. Everything the light touched was perfect.

And then something quite unexpected happened. Another change had occurred inside of her. At first, she wasn't sure of what it was—it had been so long since she had felt it. All at once, Louisa realized, it was happiness. But, this was a different kind of happiness than she'd ever felt before. This happiness came with a sense of adventure—of possibility.

How had the device come to be in the pocket of Grandpa George's coat? Was the remarkable journey into the wormhole real? Were the time travellers real? Real or not, for the time being, Louisa decided that it would be best to keep her discovery a secret.

"Mademoiselle Sparks?"

Louisa jumped at the sound of the baritone voice.

"Mademoiselle Sparks?" the cross voice repeated.

Louisa eased her head into the bedroom.

Hignard's housemaid had the neck of a bull, big muscular shoulders, bulging biceps and legs like tree trunks. She was wearing a frilly white apron with an absurdly small maid's cap perched on top of her formidable head, and her mouth was pinched into a frown.

"Mademoiselle Sparks!" the housemaid boomed a third time, stomping into the bedroom, making the floor quake.

"Yes?" Louisa reluctantly entered the room and then shakily extended a hand. "Pleased to meet you, um?"

But the maid only scowled back at her hand, as if Louisa were holding a rotting fish. "My name is Madame de Winter," she thundered. "Not, Um!" Her thin lips curled into a condescending smile.

Louisa swallowed the dry lump that had formed in her throat.

"And Mademoiselle, one o'der t'ing: do not t'ink 'zat Ah will be running around all day long tidying up after you." Madame de Winter pointed her feather duster towards the bed, where Louisa's suitcase lay open.

"I, uh—" Louisa stammered.

"Pardonne-moi? Ah am sorry, mademoiselle, but Ah do not speak ape, only Français!"

Louisa wanted to reply, *Madame, I can speak French*

perfectly well! And furthermore, Madame de Winter, you probably speak exquisite conversational ape, being that you are one, but she couldn't get a single word out.

"Monsieur 'Ig-nard will be expecting you for dinner shortly. Do not be late." With that, the maid stomped into the hall and slammed the door shut.

Louisa ran to the door and slid the latch in place. She doubted that the flimsy lock would be any match for Madame de Winter, but nonetheless it made her feel a little safer. Pressing her back against the door, she slid to the ground. The tiny bit of happiness she'd felt on the balcony had been trampled to dust.

Closing her eyes, she pictured a Saturday morning back in London. It used to be her favourite day. Saturday meant breakfast with her mother and father with buttered toast, fried eggs, rashers of bacon and piping hot tea. It also meant a long walk through Regent's Park. Louisa loved to see the giraffes from the zoo peeking at her over the fence.

Her family home was tucked into a sleepy borough of the bustling city. The house was crooked from top to bottom. The plumbing never worked quite right, and hunks of plaster were always falling off a wall or the ceiling. Afterwards, her father would declare, "This house has a bit of character," and patch them right back up again.

Despite its quirks, the rooms always felt light, warm and friendly. In the springtime, the garden was a flurry of activity, and in the late summer, Louisa's mother would make small bouquets of bellflowers, primroses and violets and place them throughout the house.

Louisa's parents were not extraordinary in any way. Her father, Henry, worked for the Underground Electric Railways Company of London. Most days he toiled away in his tiny office, in the very centre of a drab office building, where he shuffled papers from one box to another and back again. But he never complained.

Her mother, Margaret, was the opposite of Henry. Every day she woke up with a fresh idea. The trouble was that she could never quite settle on one long enough to see it through. When her mother was Louisa's age, she had wanted to be an actress. She became a teacher instead. Still, she adored the theatre. And so, her father took her to the Old Vic every year on their anniversary.

On the night of their anniversary, it had been bitterly cold. That year, the winter had lingered on into the spring. With the taxi waiting, her mother kissed Louisa on her forehead and her father gave her one of his big hugs. He looked handsome dressed in his tuxedo, even though his bow-tie was crooked, as always. And her mother was beautiful in her green dress. Her father had bought it that afternoon on his lunch break. It had cost him nearly one week's salary, but seeing her he'd declared that, "It was worth every penny." Louisa did not know why, but in the months leading up to the accident, it seemed her father had been throwing caution to the wind. It was as if he had sensed something approaching.

Louisa loved the way her father opened the door for her mother and how he held her hand as she stepped into the cab.

"Gawd! Ain't she a lovely lidy?" the cabby said upon seeing her. Things like that were always happening to her mother.

As they drove away, her mother blew Louisa a kiss through the back window and then—they were gone.

At first, she had been excited to have the whole house to herself, but soon she felt lonely. The house felt empty without her parents. Rosencrantz and Guildenstern had set a vigil for her mother and father by the front door and Louisa—as per usual—was perched in her bedroom window, searching for shooting stars. But she did not find any that night.

Instead, she watched in disbelief as two police officers walked up the drive, taking their hats off when they reached the door. There were so many things that they could have wanted, but in her heart, she knew why they had arrived.

The cabby hadn't noticed the truck until it was too

late. The road was iced over. He did not stop in time. The truck driver survived. The cabby was pronounced dead on site, and so was her father. Her mother was rushed to the hospital.

When Louisa arrived, the doctor told her that her mother did not have much longer. There was nothing more they could do. She was led to her mother's room, where she approached her bedside tentatively.

"Oh, it's you, Louisa. Silly me, I thought that you'd gone to school." Her mother spoke the words so casually as if they were standing together in their sunny garden, not a dimly lit hospital room.

"I'm here, Mum." Louisa's tears fell onto her mother's gown.

"Louisa, my darling girl." Her blue eyes shone like sapphires with flecks of green and gold, and her skin was like porcelain. In its approach, death had given her a terrible beauty. "I will always be watching over you." She squeezed Louisa's hand. As she spoke those final words, her mother stared at a point beyond her and let go.

"Goodbye," Louisa whispered.

Many times since that night, Louisa had wished that she'd delayed her parents for an instant, that she'd held on to her father for a moment more, or that she'd taken the time to tell them both just how much she loved them; anything for a few seconds delay, maybe then they would have returned to her that night. If a thousand other things had happened differently, the course of her life would have remained unchanged. But their fates had been decided.

Her thoughts turned to her grandfather, the little black cat and the two silly dogs, safe inside their yellow stone house. Louisa sighed. *I should never have come to Paris.*

∞

Fearing that she would be late for dinner, Louisa slowly opened her bedroom door and peered into the hallway, surprising a mouse that scurried along the baseboard and squeezed through a crack in the wall. A reddish light filled the lonely corridor, cluttered with Hignard's collection of oddities.

Dozens of portraits hung in the hallway, but one figure caught Louisa's attention most. At the very end of the hall was a portrait of a boy, who looked to be about her age, dressed in blue. He wore a straw hat—not the untidy, shapeless kind that Grandpa George wore, but a neat one with a green ribbon tied around it. The boy's face was as fresh as a dewdrop and although, he did not have a lumped nose or flapping red ears, Louisa knew, without a doubt, that it was most definitely Hignard.

She wandered the long corridors lined with doors that led into empty rooms and other unexpected places. Sheets were draped over most of the furnishings, and whenever she entered a new room, the powdery dust that had long sat undisturbed swirled at her feet. The whole house was a dusty, forgotten museum. And then, quite by accident, she discovered Hignard's study in the west wing of the mansion. The small, windowless chamber contained a higher concentration of peculiarities than the rest of the house as if the most unusual objects had been distilled into it.

In the far corner of the study was a brass birdcage. Inside of it was the most bedraggled beast upon which Louisa had ever laid eyes. The shabby green parrot stood as still as a stone. He had only one eye, which stared straight ahead and he was missing half of his feathers. *How gruesome*, she thought to herself. The parrot looked like he had been dead for quite some time—decades maybe. Unable to resist, Louisa stuck her finger through the bars of the cage, eager to touch one of his shiny feathers when the parrot let out a long and sorrowful cry. "*Raaaaaaaaaaaaaaaaarrrrrrrrrrrrrrp!*"

"Oh, my gosh," Louisa said, clutching her chest. "You scared me half to death."

"Beans!" the parrot cawed.

"I beg your pardon?" Louisa asked, examining the

decrepit bird through the bars of his cage.

The parrot gave a loud whistle and then repeated himself, but at a much quicker pace. "Beans! Beans! Beans!" he cawed. He gave another loud whistle and then squawked, "Bruce!"

"It's a pleasure to meet you, Bruce. My name is Louisa."

Bruce blinked and stared back at her, trying to focus his one bleary eye. He teetered from one foot to the other and then tipped towards Louisa, poking his ragged beak between the bars of the cage. Again, he cawed, but much louder, this time, "Beans! Beans! *BRUCE* wants his *BEANS!*"

Louisa surveyed the room, trying to figure out just what the bird was after. There, on the corner of Hignard's desk, was a tin full of jellybeans. Louisa took one of the green ones and held it up to the bird's mouth.

"Is this what you are looking for?" she asked.

The bird snatched the candy from Louisa's fingers, devoured it in one gulp, and gave another loud whistle.

"Beans! Bruce wants his beans!"

This time, Louisa held a purple jellybean up. Bruce refused to eat it.

"'Ze bird only likes 'ze green ones."

Louisa turned to see the corpse-faced Planchet peering over her shoulder.

"Pardonne-moi, mademoiselle, I did not mean to interrupt your, um, conversation, but 'ze dinner is about to be served."

Planchet clasped his bony hands under his chin and ushered Louisa into the dining hall. "'Zis way, mademoiselle."

Hignard was seated at the end of the dining table that spanned the entire room. At the opposite end, there was a place set for Louisa. A glittering crystal chandelier hung low over a large silver candelabrum. Rolf, Hignard's scraggly wolfhound, was spread out in front of a massive stone hearth that looked as if it had not seen a fire in decades.

"Thank goodness you've finally arrived," Hignard proclaimed. "I was beginning to think that you had gone and accepted another dinner invitation!"

I sort of wish I had, thought Louisa.

"'Ze little girl was feeding 'ze bird."

"Oh yes, ol' Brucie. I can't understand for the life of me how the daft Parrot keeps on living. Ol' Brucie must be well over two hundred years old. Of course, no one knows for sure. Perhaps it's all those green jellybeans he eats," Hignard said with a wink.

Planchet pulled out Louisa's throne-sized chair and gestured for her to sit down. Her bottom sank deep into the plush cushion.

"Well, I hope you're hungry." Hignard tied an enormous napkin around his neck.

At the mere mention of food, Louisa's stomach grumbled.

"Don't be fooled by Rolf," Hignard called, gesturing to the lanky dog slumbering by the fire. "He's an absolute beast. The other day he nearly bit the postman's leg clean off."

Rolf lazily opened an eye at the sound of his name and then resumed his nap. Louisa didn't think Rolf looked so terrible.

"I say, Planchet! What are you waiting for?" Hignard yapped. "Hop to it, man. I am practically dehydrated."

Planchet dashed into the kitchen and returned with two glasses of milk on a silver tray.

Hignard drank his glass in one gulp, spilling half of it down his chin. "Planchet, you imbecile, bring out the whole pitcher!"

Planchet was back in the dining room in an instant with the pitcher of milk. He poured Hignard a second glass.

"Stupendous. Smashing. There is nothing quite like it," Hignard blurted out between mouthfuls. "It's from my cousin Siegfried's farm in Brittany..."

But the dining table was so long that Louisa could barely understand a word that Hignard was saying.

"I'm sorry, what was that?" Louisa called down the table.

Before Hignard could reply, there was a tremor that made the cutlery rattle. Madame de Winter charged into the room with a massive pot of boiling soup, which sloshed dangerously back and forth over Louisa's head while the maid scooped it into her bowl. She then served Hignard, who started spooning the soup into his mouth just as fast as she could dish it out. Hignard licked his bowl spotlessly clean and called for the next course.

Louisa, however, had barely blown the steam off the top of her soup when Planchet cleared the table. When Madame de Winter delivered the second course, Louisa bolted upright and pinched her nose. A horrible stink had filled the air.

"My word, what is that smell?" Hignard cried. "Rolf, are you sick?"

The dog groaned at the sound of his name.

"Planchet! What have you been feeding the blasted dog?"

Madame de Winter's cackling could be heard coming from inside the kitchen.

But Hignard soon forgot about the stench permeating the dining hall and in less than ten seconds, he'd polished off his salad and was calling for more. Louisa had only eaten a single leaf of lettuce when Planchet snatched her plate. Madame de Winter came galloping back into the room with two heaping portions of caviar.

Hignard instantly gobbled his down, but Louisa wasn't quite sure what to do with hers. She'd never eaten anything like it before.

"It is jolly well delicious," Hignard proclaimed as he spooned the fish eggs directly into his mouth. "This caviar comes from the Caspian Sea, you know. Very rare, very rare, I should think that we are probably eating the absolute last batch."

When she had finally worked up enough courage to try a bite, Planchet deftly snatched her plate out from under her nose. Louisa practically leapt out of her seat when Madame de Winter plopped the next course onto the table with a thud! On her plate was a quivering gelatinous castle. The Union Jack was flying from a toothpick that jutted from one of its parapets, and the whole thing was surrounded by a moat of frogs' legs.

"It is the Battle of Waterloo, you know, with a few minor embellishments," Hignard announced. "I have it every Sunday. It's my absolute favourite."

Aspic and frog legs, YUCK!

"Don't wait for me—dig in!" Hignard mumbled with an enormous frog leg hanging out of his mouth.

Louisa examined the appendage dangling from her fork. The leg twitched, and she dropped it onto her plate, horrified. She wasn't hungry anymore.

"Don't think for a minute these frogs came from

Indonesia," Hignard proclaimed, slurping the meat off of one and throwing the bones onto the floor. "These *frogs* are *frogs* through and through. They came straight out of the Rhône."

Louisa prodded the gelatin castle with her fork. Finally, she gave up trying to eat and sat watching Hignard stuff himself.

When Hignard had cleaned the meat off of every frog leg and devoured his castle, he waved the Union Jack and called for Planchet. "Froggy! Froggy! Take our plates away! And then bring us some strawberry ice cream!"

Louisa's ears perked up, and she felt the stirrings of hunger return to her stomach. Strawberry ice cream was her absolute favourite!

Planchet gathered up the dishes and rushed to the kitchen. When he returned, he was carrying two silver cups loaded with pink ice cream.

"Spoons, Planchet! You have forgotten the blasted spoons," Hignard shrieked. "We can't be expected to eat ice cream with our fingers now, can we?"

Planchet reappeared with the spoons. Sweat poured down his face, and he was deathly pale. Indeed, he looked like he might drop dead at any moment.

"Dig in," Hignard called to Louisa.

Louisa salivated as she raised a heaping spoonful towards her mouth, but just as she was about to take her first bite, the room went dark. She heard quick footsteps crossing the room, and then another noise like a wet towel being flicked, followed by a clink as her bowl tipped onto the floor.

From across the room, a muffled thud was followed by a curse from Hignard. "Blast and botheration. I've stubbed my toe!"

More crashing and banging preceded a mournful bellow from Rolf followed by a fresh string of curses from Hignard. At last, a match was struck. Instantly, Hignard's sullen face appeared over the tiny flame. Other flames sprung from the tops of the candles as he lit them. Soon he was swinging the large candelabrum around the room and yelling for his butler.

"Planchet, you brainless wonder. Where are you? The confounded fuse has blown again. How many times do I have to remind you to get it fixed? I swear you must have the mental capacity of a common pigeon." Hignard's insults trailed off as he stomped away in search of the fuse box.

There was a SNAP! A storm of sparks rained from the ceiling. The chandelier flickered and filled the room with light. Hignard reentered the dining hall. Planchet was in close pursuit with his pants on backwards, and half of his face covered in shaving cream. Rolf was skulking behind Planchet with strawberry ice cream dripping from his whiskers.

"Just look at you, man!" Hignard shouted. "You are an utter disgrace! Sneaking off again, I see. Well, I can't say that I am surprised. Hardly anything surprises me anymore."

Louisa was set to say, *Why don't you leave Planchet alone, you big bully!* but a yawn escaped in place of words. Embarrassed, she clamped both hands over her mouth. "Sorry, Uncle Hignard. I don't mean to be rude. I'm just feeling a little sleepy. I really should get to bed."

"Yes, yes, of course, Louisa. You must be utterly drained after eating that huge meal." Hignard patted his bulging stomach. "You don't want to make yourself late for school in the morning! Perhaps we'd better head off to bed. What do you say, Planchet?"

But Planchet had already gone.

∞

Louisa dragged a chair across the bedroom floor, propped it underneath the door handle and slid the latch in place. Safely barricaded inside, she dove into bed and closed her eyes. The trip from her grandfather's, the odd incident on the train, her harrowing encounter with Madame de Winter—they all managed to make the day feel much longer than it actually was.

Louisa just wanted to go to sleep and forget about

everything, but for some reason, she could not get comfortable. Exasperated, she sat up and examined the gifts that Edward had given her. When she lifted the purple cloak, a small book slipped from its pocket. It was a journal, and not a silly pink one with heart-shaped stickers on it, either. It was the kind that one took on adventures.

Louisa untied the notebook's leather strap and skimmed through its tattered pages. Most of the hand-written notes appeared to have been composed hastily. There were splashes of ink strewn across its pages and the scrawling handwriting possessed an oddly familiar, mad rhythm. And then she found the name—Adalbert Uhrmacher—written on the final page.

The journal was part travel log, part diary—and partly filled with Adalbert's ingenious mechanical inventions. She had never read anything like it before. The contents of its pages lit her mind in ways she'd not thought possible. It was crowded with accounts of the most extraordinary places and other things that she could never have imagined. In fine detail, Adalbert had illustrated many of the rare creatures that he'd encountered on his journeys. There was an Upland Moa, a Quagga, a tortoise from the Galapagos Islands, a Dodo bird, a Caspian tiger, and even a giant squid. There were also drawings of people, friends that Adalbert had met while travelling. Some of them were wild painted men and women that looked to be from the distant past while others, it seemed, were from the far future.

Peppered throughout the journal, were bits of wisdom, and pieces of advice that Adalbert had collected on his many adventures. They were tips that one might expect a time traveller would find useful; such as, *what to pack when leaving on an expedition,* as per Sir Ernest Shackleton; or, *ten things never to do when in outer space,* by Neil Armstrong; *and how to untie a knot with your feet,* by none other than Harry "Handcuff" Houdini—each one personally autographed of course.

And then, there were the time machines. These were drawn in exacting detail. The first was a massive, intricate contraption—a literal clock tower. The devices became steadily more compact as improvements were made to the original designs. The time machine shrank from a clock tower to the size of a grandfather clock and then smaller still. The final mechanism resembled a pocket watch. Adalbert had named his masterpiece the "Parallax". Unmistakably, it was the same device that she'd found in the pocket of her grandfather's coat.

Hours slipped by, and she read well into the evening, feeling as if Adalbert was with her, whispering his secrets into her ear. Finally, with the journal perched on top of her nose—Louisa fell fast asleep—her bedroom window sending out a single square of light along the dark boulevard.

It wasn't long, however, before she was disturbed. Louisa awoke to a feint scratching sound. She propped herself up on her elbows, and the journal slid off her nose and into her lap. Squinting in the bright lamplight, she tried to locate the source of the irritating noise. She peered over the edge of her bed, eyeing the underside suspiciously. She thoroughly inspected her closet but found that it too was empty. She stepped out onto the balcony, only to find a pair of fat pigeons huddled together. Then she crept back into bed and listened some more. Feeling a little ridiculous, she switched off the light. "Go away ghosts."

For a long while there was not a sound, but then, the scratching resumed. Having thoroughly inspected her room, she opened her bedroom door just a crack and peered into the pitch-black hallway, her courage quickly fading. Steadying herself against the wall, she inched her way along the obstacle course of tables, lamps, vases and other more unexpected hazards lining the corridor. Ahead, Louisa could hear something that sounded like a grumbly snore.

"Is that you, Rolf?" she whispered.

Louisa hadn't taken three steps before her foot landed on what felt like a length of thick rope. There was a sorrowful howl.

Despite her best efforts not to, Louisa laughed. "I'm

sorry, boy, I didn't see you sleeping there." She couldn't be blamed. Rolf had sounded so dreadfully sad; it was almost comical.

It took the old wolfhound a little while to unfold his long, stiff legs and get up onto his paws. She looked up at him in surprise. To anyone else, the enormous canine might have been intimidating, but Louisa knew better.

"See now, you aren't so scary, are you, old boy?" She scratched up underneath Rolf's chin, which made his kinked tail wag and his hind leg start to thump, and so she had to stop.

Stepping lightly along the hallway, Louisa headed back towards her bedroom. She gave a quick look over her shoulder before entering and saw Rolf's big wet nose and wiry whiskers. "I suppose you want to come in, do you?"

Rolf followed her into the bedroom and plunked himself down beside the bed. Louisa's stomach rumbled and she suddenly remembered the lunch that her grandfather had packed for her.

Rolf watched with the utmost attention as Louisa cut off a piece of Brie, pressed it together with some bread and then popped the whole thing into her mouth. She tore another chunk from her baguette and stared blankly at the ceiling, so lost in thought that she didn't notice the lines of gluey drool connecting the old Wolfhound's bottom lip to the floor.

"Good old Rolf, I'd almost forgotten you were here. I'm sorry, boy; it's just that everything is in such a muddle. You see, the truth of the matter is–I don't belong here."

"Arooo?" Rolf said, which Louisa was pretty sure meant: "May I please have a taste of that delicious smelling bread, or perhaps just a bit of your cheese? Or, maybe you could squish them together and then feed them both to me at the same time?"

Louisa tore off a piece of bread. She added a hunk of cheese to it. Drool flowing–Rolf watched in high anticipation. His expression turned to pure joy when she tossed the morsel towards him, and he gulped it down.

"Arooo?" Rolf said, which assuredly meant: "I'm not sure that I even tasted that last bite, and so I was wondering if you might spare a bit more of the same stuff so that I can savour it a little this time? I promise I won't eat it so fast."

Louisa tossed Rolf another hunk of her bread and cheese, and he gulped it down just as quickly as he had the first time, maybe even quicker.

"You pig. That's all you get. I hardly have any left for myself."

Eventually, she gave up one more bite. Louisa stifled a huge yawn. Exhausted, she stretched out on her bed. "Don't worry Rolf, it'll only be for a few seconds," she promised.

As she slept, her head filled with twisted thoughts. She dreamt of an enormous eel swimming through space; its scaly body was a never-ending coil. Its horrible circular mouth opened to reveal a garden of crystal teeth that closed around her. Faces of time travellers spun about her as she slid along the eel's spiny, slime-covered tongue until she fell into the black depths of its belly.

Gradually, within the darkness, she detected a shifting black shadow. It resembled a man, except that it was much too tall and thin, with blazing red eyes. The shadow reached for her with fingers like knives. She struggled to scream but could only murmur. Her voice was locked deep inside her. She watched its monstrous frame rise over her and then vanish.

When Louisa awoke, her bedroom was filled with watery light from the brilliant moon. The wind blew in gusts, making the shutters clatter. The old house clanked and moaned, and it was so cold that she could see her breath. She pulled the covers up under her chin at the sound of footsteps coming from beyond her door. They weren't the plodding footfalls of Madame de Winter, the shuffling walk of Planchet or the deliberate plonk, plonk, plonk of her Uncle Hignard.

"Who was that, boy?" Louisa looked towards the spot where Rolf had been curled up, but he was gone. She tucked the journal into her pocket. Drawing the cloak up around her shoulders, she slipped out of bed and crept across the room. A massive shadow stretched underneath her bedroom door and then receded. "Uncle Hignard, is that you?"

Pressing her ear to the door, she could hear nothing but the creaking old house, the howling wind and the thump, thump, thump of her heartbeat. Curious as to where Rolf had wandered off to, Louisa pushed open the door and stepped into the hallway. The moonlight cut a thin, silvery pathway along the floor. A monstrous shadow spread up the wall and then sank into the stairwell. "Planchet? Madame de Winter? Rolf?" Still there was no answer.

As Louisa descended the stairs the whole house seemed to fill with a blustering wind. In the parlour, the curtains snapped in the open window. All at once, five shadows, with blazing eyes and clawed hands rose up from out of the floor, so tall that the curve of their backs pressed against the ceiling.

"Who are you? Where's Uncle Hignard?"

A hollow, inhuman sound welled up from deep inside one of the shadowy figures, "Hignard is DEAD!"

CHAPTER SIX

Quantum Entanglements

A GREAT calamitous sound like thunder and streams of light poured into Hignard's parlour through the open window, engulfing the five shadow-men in a fiery halo. Where the beams of light touched them, they began to smoke and break apart. The parlour echoed with their horrible shrieks. Louisa gasped when one of the creatures reached for her with its clawed hand and then disintegrated into dust. It was made of tiny gleaming particles that shifted and changed like desert sand.

Louisa watched helplessly. "Monsters—horrible—unbelievable—monsters!" she heard herself say.

"Recoil, shape-shifters! Perish in the light!" a deep, gargling voice pronounced. Amidst the wreckage, stood a familiar figure. Light spilled out of the golden disk that he held high above him.

Louisa shielded her eyes. Finally, when everything became still, she let her hands fall.

Amog's green-gold, reptilian eyes darted about the room while his forked tongue flicked at the air. With a movement quicker than the human eye, the amulet was tucked away, and Amog had crossed the parlour. He stood before Louisa, equal in height, but much larger in stature. The shiny, green scales covering his face and hands were like that of a medieval suit of armour. Milky white eyelids flicked over his wide almond shaped eyes. "Behold, I see that I have arrived not a moment too late. Are you harmed?" Amog placed a hand on her shoulder.

Louisa recoiled, repulsed by his three scaly fingers.

Amog's hands disappeared into the folds of his cloak.

Her voice was barely a whisper. "I'm sorry Amog, I didn't mean too—"

"Do not despair, hatchling. In my realm, you too would be a curious thing to see. Quickly now, gather your things. There is no time to waste."

"But, what about Uncle Hignard?" There was a note of despair in Louisa's voice. "The creature—it said that he was—dead."

"Hignard is not dead. He is merely in a state of deep sleep, induced by the shape-shifters."

"Oh no. Poor Hignard."

"Do not despair, hatchling, he will awaken soon."

"What were those things that attacked me?"

"It has been long since the shape-shifters have crossed into your realm. Banished from this world, centuries ago, they could materialize only as shadows, night terrors, stalking the dreams of children. But there is no doubt now that our ancient enemy, the Nephilim, have returned."

Louisa shook her head, trying to make some sense out of what he was saying. "Crossed into my realm? Crossed from where?"

"The Nephilim dwell in an empire of shadow, a terrifying place thought to be sealed off from this world forever."

Louisa recalled what Rhadamanthus had said. "But, I thought that the Nephilim were from Atlantis?"

"Yes, hatchling. Nevertheless, that is but a small part of the story. The Nephilim are descendants of the first men, master builders, scientists and philosophers. It was they who founded the ancient city of Atlantis."

"How can the Nephilim be human when their bodies are made from sand?"

"Not sand, hatchling—diamonds. In the beginning, they were men—" Amog scanned the room. "But explanations must come later. Do you have your time machine?"

Louisa's eyebrows knit together when she reached into her pocket. *Oh no! My goodness, no! The time machine is missing.* She hastily searched her other pockets, without success. Fearing that Amog would think her too careless to be a time traveller, Louisa patted her side. "I have it right here," she lied, far too embarrassed to admit that she'd lost it.

"Quickly, hatchling, go to the window."

"Now what?" The bottom rung of a rope ladder dropped down in front of her nose. Louisa suspected that she would not be returning to Hignard's house any time soon—if ever.

"Hunts-up, fair lady!" Rhadamanthus called from above. The spritely scientist was clinging to the peak of the steep roof, craning his neck over the side.

"If it's not too much trouble, could you let out a little more slack? Please!" she called up to him, and the ladder released with a jolt.

Louisa's palms were slick with sweat as she dangled from the bottom rung. She kicked at the air, trying desperately to get a foothold. The wind was knocking her about considerably. Broken pieces of slate slid onto the lawn far beneath her as the craft teetered dangerously overhead.

Amog's head poked out of the window. "I am here, hatchling, do not fret."

Rhadamanthus offered up his hand when Louisa finally boarded the craft. "Luck abounds! I feared that we had searched for you in vain." Taking a step back, he adjusted his monocle, to admire her purple cloak. "Great wonder, much has come to pass since we first met, not yet one day ago. Alas, ye are clothed as a true time traveller."

From this vantage point, Louisa could see the whole of Paris glistening in the early morning sun. "It's beautiful," she whispered.

"To be sure, it is a sight to remember for the rest of your days." Amog leapt into the time machine. "But, we must hasten at once to a safer place, indeed, if such a thing can be found in these evil times. Even inside the never-ending paths of the abyss, we shall not be free from danger."

"Where are the others?" Louisa asked.

"The time travellers are scattered like sheep. Some are hiding and some, I fear, are killed."

"Hark! The varlets have returned." Rhadamanthus pointed towards three Nephilim gathered together at the foot of the house. "Alas, a second more and all wouldst've been lost."

Louisa peered over the roof's edge. "What do they want with me?"

"The Nephilim seek the time travellers, my lady." Rhadamanthus checked a dial and then tapped at one of the crystals that had gone dim. The crystal began to glow brightly once more, and the craft shifted from its resting place, floating upwards.

"But why?" she asked.

"To extinguish them."

Louisa snuck a jellybean into her mouth just as the world around her slowed and then stopped and fell away.

Clinging to the edge of the craft, she looked out into the endless abyss. "Belthazzar." The name slipped from her lips along with a puff of cold air. "He is responsible for this, isn't he?"

"Perhaps my lady." Rhadamanthus's fingers sped over the console, and the craft emerged into a tunnel of gigantic proportions. "Though, we cannot be certain."

"What will we do, Rhadamanthus?"

"Amog and I must find the remaining time travellers—if there are, indeed, any left to find. They are the key to unravelling this mystery."

"I can help."

"Nay, my lady," Rhadamanthus replied. "I forbid you

to aid us in this perilous quest."

"Rhadamanthus, let me help you—please."

"'Tis certain you are brave, but Methinks, you should be practicing letter writing, needlework and catching boys, not catching villains, nay."

Louisa's cheeks burned, but her anger turned to despair. *I guess it's just the same. I was never meant to be a time traveller. Now that the time machine is lost, I can go back to being a regular person.* But, as she made this last confession, she looked at the sign of the lemniscate etched into her golden ring and knew that she could never again be a regular person.

Rhadamanthus seemed to be engaged in a ferocious inner debate. Finally, his eyebrows froze and then floated upwards. "Forgive me, my lady," he said with a long breath. He looked at Louisa as a kindly father might look upon a daughter. "'Tis oft' the smallest alterations giveth rise to strikingly great consequences."

"Does this mean—I can stay?"

Amog raised a type of telescope to his eye. "It seems we're in this together now, hatchling."

"What do you see, Amog?" Rhadamanthus sounded quite anxious.

"The scope has located a ripple in the space-time continuum, but no tidal waves. To be sure, someone is meddling with the timeline, but whatever mischief he is planning, it has not yet fully come to pass."

Louisa edged closer to Rhadamanthus. "That last bit, what did Amog mean by it?"

"Aye, my lady, the scope can detect even minor alterations to the timeline." Rhadamanthus was speaking in fits, frantically looking in every direction, while adjusting the levers; foot peddles and dials inside of the time machine. "When the past is altered, there is a ripple effect on the space-time continuum, mostly, with little consequence. Alas, on occasion, a surge of tidal forces is unleashed, causing untold alterations to the past, present and future."

"Finicky, finicky," Amog grumbled while adjusting the time-scope. "I believe, there is still a chance to avoid the disruption—but we must not sit on our hands. The coordinates suggest the disturbance will originate somewhere in the southwestern region of what is known in this age as Denmark. I estimate the time of origin, by the Gregorian calendar, to be the year sixteen forty-one, month eleven, day nine, the time of day—not yet discernable."

Rhadamanthus thumped the dashboard with his hat nearly sending them spiraling out of control. "Fie! I fear the witch is in mortal danger."

"I concur." Amog tucked the time-scope away into the folds of his cloak. "Set the co-ordinates for Denmark, year sixteen forty-one."

NOVEMBER 9th. 1641

Town of Rÿpen,

Denmark

The sun had begun to dip in the grey sky. A murder of crows squawked noisily to one another from the bare branches of a large beech tree. More of the black birds settled along the ruined walls of the moated castle, Riberhus, that lay on the outskirts of the medieval town of Rÿpen–to spy on the throngs of townspeople gathering. Brightly painted canvases hanging from the crumbling castle walls portrayed a bent, warted hag being burned at the stake, her eyes piously turned upwards, while the exalted townspeople looked on.

"I don't see Brünnhilde," Louisa whispered.

She and Rhadamanthus were carefully hidden along the parapet wall, observing the assembly.

"She is yonder. Though, you may not know her. She is, perhaps, not many seasons older than you, my lady."

Cheeks stained with grime and tears; a young woman, with a proud fair face, was thrust into the centre of the mob, where preparations for a bonfire were hastily being made. A ladle was lifted to her mouth. She drank from it and then spit at the leering townspeople.

"Burn, witch!" a sour faced woman called out.

Others echoed her call.

"Rhadamanthus, do you know what they are saying?"

"Aye, my lady, though, I will only say that 'tis ill tidings for Brünnhilde."

A bag of gunpowder was strapped to Brünnhilde's back

and a man wearing a black clerical hat, stepped onto on a platform that stood high above the throngs of townspeople.

"The Magistrate has arrived!" the same sour faced woman proclaimed.

"'Tis he." Rhadamanthus' voice was a gruff whisper. "Belthazzar has fopped us. He is no friend. Nay, he is our gravest foe."

Belthazzar stood tall and cruel over the assembly; his somber face predicted doom. He produced a scroll and then read aloud from it. "By order of his Majesty, the righteous King Clovis XV, you Brünnhilde Grumm are sentenced to burn for the practice of black magic, against Didrik the Tailor." Belthazzar motioned towards a stooped, green-eyed man, with an oily, jealous face. "Didrik claims to have been awoken in the night by *you* Brünnhilde and three other witches, who held him to his bed while you poured a potion into his mouth."

At Belthazzar's cue, a ladder was dragged into the clearing. The fire was lit, and the mob stepped back as the flames crackled to life.

Brünnhilde screamed at the sight of it. "It is a lie," she pleaded. "Tell them Didrik, how you have lied. You have always been envious of my husband who is a successful businessman, but you—you are a wretch who drinks from morning to night in our tavern and cannot pay. Tell them the truth, you vile, black-hearted man!"

Didrik shifted nervously from foot to foot. "Say what you will, woman," he sneered. "These things always end in the same way—fire."

The villagers stood tightly packed together, swaying shoulder to shoulder, with eyes greedy for what was soon to come.

Belthazzar continued his sentencing. "Cursed by Brünnhilde during the night, the following day Didrik fell ill! From that time forth, his luck steadily dwindled, until he was forced, just last week, to close his workshop."

There was a gasp amongst the townspeople and Brünnhilde was roughly thrown down onto the ladder. Her wrists and ankles were tied to its rungs. "It is you who will burn, Didrik!" she cried. "You and the others who have stood by and done nothing while an innocent woman dies." Brünnhilde was lifted high into the air, her silhouette black against the smoky sun. A tense silence fell over the townspeople. Only the crows could be heard cawing to one another. And then, with a boisterous cheer, the ladder was tossed forward.

As the ladder tilted towards the fire, it began to bounce, ever so slightly, in a way that suggested someone was climbing it. The rope binding Brünnhilde's hands and feet sprung apart, as if on its own accord. The sack of gunpowder dropped from her back into the flames. The fire emitted a screeching noise when the sack of gunpowder lit and then exploded with a *CRACK!* There was a brief flash of light, just before the ladder fell into the blaze—empty.

∞

Amog's disembodied head hovered in the centre of the room, and his forked tongue flicked the air. Next, his broad shoulders materialized and finally his chest became visible, when his scales stabilized. Quickly donning his cloak, he stood with the others inside a tiny cottage, hidden away in the midst of a dense forest.

Rhadamanthus clapped his hands. "Marvellous! To think, such a thing truly exists, a cloak of invisibility. Amog, I should like to see it closer if you would only allow it."

Amog moved his hand in a slow arc. As if by magic, his scales took on the attributes of the room, causing his arm to melt into the background. "I do not require such trinkets."

Rhadamanthus, the prototypical scientist, leaned in for a closer look. "Astonishing, your scales provide a natural camouflage. We must travel to Erras, together. Oh, what a spectacle your world must be."

Amog made a terrifying grin, revealing a mouth full of long, pointy teeth that stuck out in every direction. "One day, perhaps, in better times, Rhadamanthus. It would gladden my three hearts to feast my eyes upon the magnificent twin moons of Erras and to feel the warmth of her green sun—"

"Imp! Gargoyle! Get back!" Brünnhilde, who had up to that point been standing in the room utterly stupefied, instantly became violently animated.

Cautiously, Louisa approached the panic-stricken girl, in an attempt to comfort her. "Brünnhilde! It's me—Louisa."

With a wild look in her eyes, Brünnhilde snatched a broomstick off the wall and thrashed it about the tiny cottage.

Rhadamanthus moved in front of Louisa, at the ready for whatever Brünnhilde might hurl at them. "She does not know you, my lady. For it will be long before you meet."

Brünnhilde leveled her broomstick at Amog. "'Vat are you? Serpent? Man? Demon?" she hissed.

Amog, with his amulet in hand, raised his arm and replied, "Friend. Though, I warn you, witch. Do not make us enemies."

Rhadamanthus stretched his arms out like a referee. "We are, all of us, your friends."

A hint of a smile appeared on Brünnhilde's lips, and Amog's arm fell to his side. "Is it safe to approach?"

Brünnhilde's eyes narrowed. "I suppose."

Amog inched towards her sideways. "If I do, you must promise to remain calm." He continued his sidelong shuffle until he was standing directly in front of her. "I am Amog." He cautiously extended a hand to Brünnhilde, who in turn, cautiously took it.

"I am Brünnhilde," she replied. "But, I suspect 'zat you knew 'zis already."

Brünnhilde set out several slices of a spiced pie along with a large jug full of pickled eggs and apples. The time travellers were gathered tightly around the kitchen table. "How did you find 'zis place?"

"We have been observing you for some time," Amog confessed.

"For 'vut purpose, demon?" Brünnhilde tended to the kettle that hissed over the little wood-burning stove.

"To save you," Louisa insisted.

"And now you must flee, leaving behind everything, even your name." Amog gratefully accepted his odorous tea. Taking a sip, he nodded approvingly. "No one must know that you have survived the fire. Brünnhilde Grumm of Rÿpen is dead. I advise you to think again, before carelessly laying curses—even upon wretches like Didrik, the tailor." Amog continued to explain everything that had transpired up to the moment that he had camouflaged himself, scaled the ladder and snatched Brünnhilde from the flames. "We suspect that Belthazzar is hunting the time travellers."

"'Zis Belthazzar, you say, he and 'ze Magistrate are one in 'ze same?" Brünnhilde slipped a bit of crust into the mouth of a much littler Harold the rat, who peeked out from her pocket.

"Aye, Brünnhilde. It seems the villain has many guises." Unhinging his jaws, Amog tossed three pickled eggs into his cavernous mouth.

While Rhadamanthus, Brünnhilde and Amog delved further into conversation, Louisa's mind wandered. She was, after all, still a young girl and unused to such seriousness. She followed a little bat that fluttered amongst the strings of onions and garlic hanging from the ceiling and then nestled into a hole above the bookshelf. Many books lined the shelves of Brünnhilde's library, but not the usual sort you would find in a modern day store. These books were large and very old, with musty, worn leather bindings bearing cryptic symbols.

Mingled in amongst the volumes in this eccentric library was an assortment of abnormalities preserved inside curiously shaped glass jugs of embalming fluid. Inside one jar was the cat-sized corpse of a monstrous spider. Louisa shivered at the sight of it floating in the cloudy, greenish liquid. But she soon forgot about the spider, when the soft notes of a strange and sweet song drifted in through the window.

"Thistle and sage and nettles grow.
As you and I and anyone know;
Horestale, hyssop and brambles sprout,
We yank their stems and snatch them out!"

Louisa peeked through the strands of greying moss that dangled above the entrance of the cottage. Snowflakes filtered down through the tangled treetops. Despite the frigid temperatures, delicate flowers bloomed just below the surface of the icy stream. Beyond the stream, three old women treaded through the forest, singing while they plucked the mushrooms that sprang up from the frozen ground to meet them.

"Be cautious child. 'Ze witches are not nearly as frail as 'zey look," Brünnhilde whispered.

Rhadamanthus knelt before Louisa. "My lady, we must prepare. 'Tis time we left this place."

"Are we going home?" Louisa's question was unexpectedly tinged with sadness. "Wherever that may be."

"Alas, we must find Radicon, before the villain Belthazzar does." Adjusting his monocle, Rhadamanthus examined Louisa with some concern. "Take heart, my lady, for our adventures have only just begun."

NOVEMBER 5th, 2290

Covent Garden,

London, England

"Dear me." Radicon magnified his gaze to four hundred, zooming in on the mob gathering outside of his cluttered antique shop. The thin strip of sky visible over the city was bumper-to-bumper with hover-cars stuck in the afternoon rush. Glowing electronic eyes could be seen through the barred windows of a hover-bus with the word RECYCLING written across its side in stark lettering. Reporter-drones circled high above the congested traffic.

The store window rang out when a bottle struck it, causing a web-like fracture. "Cybrid trash!" a man bellowed.

"Parasite! Job thief!" a woman screeched.

One after another, violent images flashed above Radicon's holovision set. Underneath, a steady stream of headlines rushed through the air.

—Anti-Robot Violence Flares Up in London, Paris, and New York City.

—All Robots Must Carry Identity Cards.

—Robots Banned From English Civil Service.

—Robot Labour Camp Opens In East London.

"And now a word from a prominent Member of Parliament and leader of the Anti-Robot League." The reporter's voice was devoid of emotion.

A three-dimensional hologram of a man with curious star-shaped irises materialized inside the room. He appeared to stare menacingly at Radicon. "All robot-kind are our enemy. We will not be safe until each and every last cybrid is dismantled and sold off for spare parts."

The window rattled when a brick struck it, causing the glass to split. Radicon paced the narrow aisle of his store, wringing his hands. "Goodness, this doesn't seem right."

A burst of light preceded a catastrophic noise that came from inside of the antique shop. "Dear me, it seems that I'm surrounded." With a click and a whir, Radicon's head rotated one hundred and eighty degrees. "Rusty gussets!" He focussed in on the four hooded figures standing inside of a massive sled that was, to his dismay, firmly wedged amongst his precious antiques.

"In approximately seven seconds the store window will be smashed, an angry mob will rush inside, and you will be pulled to pieces and then sold off for spare parts," came a deep, gargling voice.

Without further consultation, Radicon was hauled into the sled, and they vanished.

It was getting quite crowded in Rhadamanthus' tipsy craft. On more than one occasion, Louisa could have floated away if Amog had not snatched her out of the air. Both Louisa and Brünnhilde clung on to the weighty mechanical man to stop from being pitched over the side into the wormhole.

"Hunts-up, fair ladies!" Rhadamanthus yelped, right before the time machine passed underneath a type of archway and then sailed around a corner landing both Louisa and Brünnhilde upside down and backwards in their seats.

"I vould have better luck riding my broomstick," Brünnhilde complained.

Amog lifted the time-scope to his eye and grew silent. He then handed it to Louisa and motioned for her to look through its lens.

Louisa squinted an eye and peered into the scope, instantly seeing herself aboard a passenger train.

"It is merely an illusion," Amog assured her.

Louisa recognized the rectangular patches of green and mustard yellow fields. She watched a lovely old stone barn pass by. Its slumped roof was the colour of rain clouds. Next to it, the earth had swallowed up half of a tractor's rusted shell. The purple silhouette of the Pyrenees Mountains loomed in the distance. She was on her way back to Grandpa George's village.

The train crossed over a bridge and rushed headlong into a tunnel. The cabin lights wavered. Louisa watched her watery reflection in the window. When the train emerged from the tunnel, streams of sand beat against the windowpanes and the sun shone much harsher. In the time it had taken the train to travel through the tunnel, the pleasant scenery had become a vast grey dessert. Swaths of shoddy homes dotted the landscape. Most were built with scraps of wood, tin and haphazardly laid brick. Mountains of plastic containers glinted in the sunlight. Dozers spewing grimy smoke lumbered through the piles of waste. A few forlorn individuals looked up at the sound of the passing train. They were mere shadows of humans flitting amongst the dirt. They looked to be the condemned—the living dead.

In the distance, a row of enormous conical shaped concrete structures lined the horizon. A thin jet of smoke rose from the centre of one of the buildings that had been blackened as if by a tremendous fire. An unwholesome air hung about the monolith and nothing stirred in all of the barren lands that surrounded it. Something bad had happened—something big.

Louisa lowered the time-scope and passed it to Amog with a trembling hand. "What does it mean, Amog?"

"The time-scope has shown you an eventuality—a potential outcome—resulting from a single alteration to the past. This change, if it comes to pass, will set in motion a series of cataclysmic events. The incident is predicted to occur in the year two thousand and twelve, month eight, day one, hour twenty, minute seven, second twenty, of the Gregorian calendar. It will take place in the south of France, in a place called Jardin."

SEPTEMBER 2nd, 2012

The Catacombs,

14th arrondissement,

Paris, France

CHAPTER SEVEN

The Saboteur

GENDUN GLANCED over his shoulder before entering the lonely passageway that led into the abandoned train station. Weeds grew through fissures in the pavement, and the walls were crisscrossed with graffiti. A smoldering pile of garbage was the only source of light in this section of the underground. Long ago, the power had been cut permanently. There were many places like this in Paris, where no real people ever went. *Real people* were what Gendun called those who lived on the surface, those who had homes and jobs and families with children who had friends and went to school.

Inside of the squalid passageway, a beggar crouched on the floor. The lines crossing her face were filled with grime and her bare head was browned from years of living under the sun. It was difficult to imagine that she'd ever been a child. The remnants of that youth had gone. The old woman stared blankly at him with her opaque eyes. A whisper escaped her sunken mouth. Gendun dropped in his last few coins and hurried on his way.

Raising the makeshift torch that he had snatched from the fire, he continued onwards into the catacombs stacked high with human bones. It was rumoured that even the most stouthearted who walked through the abysmal hallways had fallen to their knees and wept at the sight. The dead, however, did not bother him. He'd found it was the living that caused most of his troubles.

Gendun counted out one hundred paces and stopped. Standing very close to the wall, he ran his fingers over the skulls, searching for a break, just as he had been shown. Without foreknowledge, it would be impossible for a passerby to notice the entryway existed. It was skillfully disguised using elements of scale and matching the pattern of skulls and bones from the fore wall to the rear wall. The faultless optical illusion made the opening almost invisible. He found an edge and sidestepped through the hidden entrance.

Following the trail of water that trickled along

the milky floor, he travelled gradually downwards. On occasion, he would stop where the wall opened up into a deep well or glimmering cavern and feel the extraordinary device through his coat and listen to its ticking. With something like this in his possession, he could make an unlimited fortune. He would become a world famous magician—a real one, not a fake like the rest. Or, better yet, he would be the most notorious bank robber in history!

For months, he'd been biding his time, playing along, waiting patiently for the perfect opportunity. But for some reason, he'd passed on several favourable opportunities to steal the time machine from Adalbert. More than once, he'd had it in his hands, with nothing to stop him from getting away. He cursed himself when the old man went missing. He feared Adalbert's sudden disappearing act had ruined his plans altogether. But then, miraculously, he'd recognized a very particular device in the Café Papillon, right before Louisa tucked it away into her coat.

He'd seen only its edge, but that had been enough; he immediately knew what it was. He would be halfway across time before the silly girl noticed that it was gone. There was just one problem—he was missing the instruction manual. He'd looked everywhere for Adalbert's journal, but it was not in any of the old man's usual hiding places. Without it, the time machine was useless to him. He had witnessed enough time travel related catastrophes to know that one should never, under any circumstances, simply press a button.

Usually, resolving a setback of this magnitude would have been foremost on his mind. But, there was something else troubling him at the moment, namely, the look on Louisa's face when he'd first met her in the café. He had often seen the same look; each time he accidentally caught a glimpse of himself in a mirror. It was an expression of the most profound loneliness. Gendun clenched his fist. Pity was an indulgence that he could not afford.

He emerged from a spiral staircase into a cavern and then crossed an ancient stone bridge that led to a gate.

"Human child, why have you come to this place?" the guard hissed.

It took Gendun a moment to find his voice. "I have matters to discuss with Belthazzar," he piped. The Nephilim always made him a bit twitchy.

A heavy chain shifted, and the iron-latticed gate began to rise. Obediently, Gendun followed the guard deep into the fortress through a warren of torch-lit corridors. He was left alone in a windowless gallery crowded with extraordinary artifacts. To his surprise, he recognized Theoderic's gauntlet, Alpharabius' obsidian skull, Sigermus' golden book and da Vinci's winged time machine. *What has Belthazzar done?*

"You have come just in time, boy." Belthazzar stood in front of an ornate mirror with his back turned so that just his face was visible in its silvery reflection. His translucent skin was pulled tight over his angular cheekbones, and deep red circles underlined his eyes.

He beckoned to Gendun with his skeletal fingers. "Come, stand by my side, for we have much to discuss." Drawing him close, Belthazzar whispered into his ear. "Did you know that the Prince of Wallachia used to dine while his enemies were slowly crushed beneath him?" Belthazzar stroked the edge of a long dining table that had been built on top of a wide press. There were other apparatuses inside the room as well, terrifying ones of a more sinister nature. "Do not let my fascination with the macabre disturb you. It is just one of my many little hobbies, nothing more. Tell me, boy, do you have any pastimes?"

Gendun shook his head.

"No? Why, everyone has an interest, some small fascination. Take this wonderfully morbid instrument for instance. Do you not find it captivating?" Belthazzar stroked the chin of the evil looking iron helmet. "It is called a gossip's bridle. Once screwed in place, the mask is impossible to remove. It is intended to keep the tongue from wagging. There is nothing more infuriating than someone who doesn't know how to keep his mouth shut.

Wouldn't you agree?" Like a lion, Belthazzar advanced upon Gendun, who staggered back from him, as if at any moment the helmet might be clapped onto his head forever. "But enough about my little hobby. I understand that you are a thief? Not a petty thief, but a professional one. Am I correct?"

Gendun nodded eagerly. "I am." Though, he quickly changed his tone. "Well, you see—that is to say—I was... once a thief." His instincts told him that Belthazzar was playing a careful game. To him, a twitch of an eyebrow, the dilation of a pupil, the tremor of a lip—spoke volumes more than words ever could.

Belthazzar's eagle eye fell on Gendun. "I also understand that you are somewhat of a saboteur."

Gendun laughed uneasily. "Yes, I suppose that is also true, but I gave it up, to be Adalbert's apprentice."

"And where, may I ask, is Adalbert now?" Belthazzar's silky voice was beginning to sound a little exaggerated.

"I am not sure. No one is."

"And what if I were to propose that you took on one final job? You see, I am looking for someone to make a simple alteration to the guidance system of Rhadamanthus' time machine, without his knowledge of course. Surely, this would be an easy task for an individual with your special talents."

"Sorry Belthazzar, sabotage is no longer in my

repertoire," Gendun replied. It was clear to him now what Belthazzar was up to.

"And what if I were to say that I know precisely where Adalbert is being held and that his very survival depends upon your acceptance of my request?"

Gendun had not expected this.

"What was that, boy? I did not hear your reply?" Belthazzar cocked an ear in his direction. There was a deadly note in his voice. "What is that ticking? I have heard it ever since you walked into this room."

"Ticking?" Gendun's hands disappeared into his drooping pockets. *Très stupide!* Silently, he cursed himself for bringing the time machine with him.

"Answer me, you little filth!" Belthazzar's hand came to rest on the bulbous head of a twisted cane. "I am warning you, boy, I have ways of finding things out."

"It is nothing," Gendun insisted.

Belthazzar's eyes narrowed into two red slits. "You miserable rodent, show me the contents of your coat!" He raised his cane to strike Gendun.

"You must be referring to these." With a trembling hand, Gendun peeled back his sleeve to expose no less than nineteen wristwatches fastened along his reedy arm, all of them going *tick-tock, tick-tock, tick-tock!* "I am, what you might call, a watch aficionado," he said slyly.

Belthazzar's cane dropped to the floor with a clatter.

A jackal's grin parted his lips. "Come, Gendun, whisper to me what you desire most. Do not hold back. For, there is no limit to what I can provide. Do what I ask, and the finer things in life can be yours at last. But first, I must warn you, do not make the grave mistake of betraying me." Belthazzar snatched Gendun up by the shirt collar and lifted him until only his toes touched the floor. "For, if you do, I promise that you will rot in my dungeon until you have forgotten everything, even your name. You will know only misery. Not even death will have the power to relieve your suffering."

SEPTEMBER 1st, 2012

The Village of Jardin,

Southern France

CHAPTER EIGHT

Night and Fog

LIGHTNING FLASHED, illuminating Grandpa George's little house. Thunder sounded with a *BOOM!* Louisa drew her cloak tighter. She caught a glimpse of Ms. Nickel's before the cat leapt from the wall into the garden.

"There." Amog pointed towards the house.

Brünnhilde saw it next. "Demon," she hissed.

As if in a dream, Louisa heard Rhadamanthus say, "Hark! The Nephilim are at hand. Look away, my lady. You must not see yourself."

The Nephilim scaled the wall towards her bedroom window like a giant spider. Its arms and legs stretched out in impossibly thin strands.

Louisa's double stared nervously out into the gloom from inside of the house. The window went dark. Louisa remembered how she had ducked down with her knees pulled up close to her thumping chest.

"Quickly, Amog, you must do it now." Rhadamanthus was in a panic.

Amog raised the amulet. There was a tremendous thundering sound. Brilliant sparks lit up the house as bright as day. The sky was a vast ceiling of rolling clouds, illuminated pink by the surges of light. The Nephilim let out a sound like howling wind and then disintegrated into a hail of gleaming particles.

"Get down." Amog crouched alongside the garden wall.

Louisa flattened herself against the wall next to Amog and Brünnhilde. "That was close."

"Too close, hatchling." Making an adjustment to the time-scope, Amog peered into its lens. "Something eludes me; I am sure of it."

Rhadamanthus settled next to Louisa. "Methinks, 'tis best not to linger in this place too long."

But Louisa wished that she could rush inside to see Grandpa George and the two silly dogs. She would give them each a big tearful hug, and they would gather around the kitchen table to hear about her remarkable adventures.

Walking rather stiffly, Radicon was the last to join them. "Yes, I wholeheartedly agree. I believe that I am in need of a recharge."

"Silence." Amog crawled to the far corner of the garden wall.

Two more of the Nephilim had appeared. One twisted itself along a bough of the old oak tree in the yard, and the other scaled the trunk in slow liquid movements. Amog took aim with his amulet and leapt high into the air. The tree was captured in a halo of dazzling light. With a splintering crack, its trunk was cut in two and then fell smoldering onto the lawn. Curling under the amulet's fire like two burning wicks, the Nephilim dissolved into glittering ash.

"Is it over?" Louisa asked.

The sight of Amog's milky white eyes startled Louisa, as his massive head emerged from over the wall. He made one of his terrifying thorny grins. "It seems we are safe for now, hatchling." His hands suctioned to the surface of the wall, and he slithered onto its edge and stopped. From behind Amog, the shifting particles of the Nephilim glided around his neck like a tentacle and lifted him into the air. His scales changed from green to icy blue as he fought against the creature's grasp.

"Amog!" Louisa's cry was drowned out by thunder. Unable to reply, Amog only stared back at her with eyes full of sadness and awe. His limbs had frozen solid, and he ceased to struggle.

The air around Louisa seemed to charge. Rhadamanthus steadied himself on one knee, taking careful aim at the Nephilim with a type of electronic gun. For an instant, the air solidified, and it was as if they were underwater. There was a tremor and then a burst of lightning shot from the gun. She was knocked to the ground, and her head exploded with pain.

When Louisa awoke, she could tell by the pale light that it was nearly dawn. The rain had stopped, but she was chilled to the bone. She rubbed her arms to stave off the dampness and then blew into her hands to stop the sting of the biting cold. She had nearly forgotten about the cool, damp weather that was so particular to the early mornings in the south of France. They were not far from Grandpa George's house, perhaps only a few miles. Brünnhilde, Radicon and Rhadamanthus were gathered together under a grouping of trees, near the edge of a pond. She knew this place. It was where her grandfather had taught her to fish. The time travellers bowed their heads, and Rhadamanthus spoke in a somber tone as if he was saying a prayer.

As she reached the sandy shoreline, the rain was tapering off into a fine mist. The time travellers were gathered around Amog, blinking away their tears and the rain. Amog was wrapped in his purple cloak with his amulet clasped to his chest. He rested, partly submerged, a short ways out from the waters edge. His scales had not yet lost their bluish tinge, and his eyes were closed.

"Rhadamanthus, what has happened to Amog?"

"My lady, I can hardly say, it pains me so. Amog, our protector, has fallen to the Nephilim. The devil lay in hiding just beyond the wall and in a surprise attack, froze his blood. And I, in my folly, did not act quickly enough. Alas, I killed the Nephilim, but I did not save our dear friend, Amog." Rhadamanthus' face twisted into an expression of utter sorrow. "Oh, how I have failed."

"But, Rhadamanthus, we can't just leave him here."

"Nay, my lady, Amog must be returned to the water before sunrise. 'Tis the sacred right of all Errians of Royal blood." Straightening himself, Rhadamanthus walked out into the pond. He took hold of Amog's frigid body and pushed him away.

A large stone latched to Amog's side carried him down under the murky water to rest amongst the reeds. "We will return for you, my valiant friend when all is set right. Together, we shall travel to Erras, though you shall never again feel the warmth of her green sun.

May the eye of Horus watch over you, time traveller."
Despondently, Rhadamanthus checked the time-scope.
"Alas, we must go."

∞

"Something is amiss," Rhadamanthus said from
inside the time machine. "'Tis as though someone has
tampered with the controls."

Louisa noticed someone or something stirring at
the base of a tree near by. She cupped her hands to her
mouth. "Rhadamanthus!"

The faint light of his lamp fell over her. "Hurry, my
lady. We are about ready to depart."

Rhadamanthus frantically checked and double-
checked the controls. "'Tis complete chaos, an absolute
tangle, an utter discombobulation!" He vigorously
massaged his temples and then made some further
adjustments to the dials and levers. "Shall we be off?"

Radicon looked skeptical. "Are you certain,
everything is well?"

Rhadamanthus held his finger to the ignition switch.
"Quite so."

"Wait!" came a tiny voice from just beyond the
clearing.

"Gendun?" Louisa asked, puzzled.

But, she had already began to crinkle and collapse. And then bit-by-bit, her body rematerialized, but when she opened her eyes, she was not where she'd expected to be.

SEPTEMBER 2ⁿᵈ, 2012

Somewhere under

the district of Montparnasse,

14ᵗʰ arrondissement,

Paris, France

Louisa was locked inside a dank and dimly lit chamber. Quivering red light filtered in from the edges of the door. Slowly, her eyes adjusted to the four walls that closely surrounded her. She struggled to free her wrists, but the cords were expertly knotted. The air stirred—as if a breath had drifted out of the shadows. She was not alone. A vicious, dripping snarl came from the opposite corner of the cell, where an immense black creature with long fangs crouched.

"Rolf!" she exclaimed when the old Wolfhound bounded towards her. Louisa could never have thought that being slobbered on by a dog could feel so uplifting. "How on earth did you get in here, boy? And where is Uncle Hignard?"

Her cheerfulness faded as grim reality set in and a host of desolate thoughts welled up inside of her. *If only I could be rid of this wretched, tiresome, uncomfortable adventure. I wish it were Saturday morning, and I was back at home in London, having breakfast around our kitchen table. I have made an absolute mess of everything.*

Then something quite extraordinary happened; instead of feeling timid and soft on the inside, she felt hardened and more than a little angry and mostly determined to break free and find the other time travellers. Louisa reexamined the impenetrable walls and door. "Oh Rolf, it's impossible." Then it occurred to her that Adalbert's journal was still in her pocket and that its pages contained every sort of useful recommendation designed to help time travellers cope with sticky situations.

Rolf snarled, and the fur bristled along the ridge of his back at the sound of slow and heavy footsteps echoing from outside. A menacing shadow reached underneath the door.

"Who's there?" Louisa called timidly, not feeling as brave as she had moments earlier.

A slat snapped opened. "Welcome."

Louisa's courage wavered for an instant until she found her voice. "Rogvolod, where are my friends?" she bleated. But the slat was snapped shut without a reply.

Rolf made another low growl before unleashing a loud WOOF! Rogvolod's shadow flittered beneath the door and then slipped away.

"Good boy, Rolf." *Now, let's get to work.* She leaned forward and shook her shoulders until the journal fell to the floor. Using her nose to leaf through its pages, Louisa stopped at the name, Harry "Handcuff" Houdini. "Let's see—*making an elephant vanish; escaping from an underwater box; removing handcuffs;* here it is—*untying a knot with your feet.*"

Louisa carefully studied the diagram. She then rolled onto her back, made a loop with her arms and squeezed her legs through. Just like Houdini, she used her toes like fingers to pick at the knot. With a bit of a struggle, the cords fell from her wrists.

But it was a man named Archimedes who gave her the vital information that was required to break open the door. Louisa stood back to admire her handiwork. By threading her cloak through the slat, she had managed to lasso the door handle. Next, she tightly coiled the other end of the cloak and looped it over a stone that jutted from the inside wall, to create a rudimentary pulley.

"Give me a lever long enough and a point on which to place it, and I shall move the world," Louisa softly declared, as she swung from the cloak. Dust shot from the hinges as the door moved slightly upwards, leaving her dangling. On the third attempt, the door swung up off its hinges and fell to the floor with a clatter.

When I am through with this nasty business, I will add, removal of hopelessly locked doors, to Adalbert's journal.

"Time to go." Louisa tugged on Rolf's collar, but he would not budge. "Come on boy!" She tried again, but he was leaning stubbornly back on his haunches. "Here, boy!" Louisa pleaded. "I know." Louisa scratched up underneath Rolf's scraggly chin and whispered very softly to him. "We have to go now, Rolf. We have to find the other time travellers. Do you understand?"

Reluctantly, Rolf stood and gave a bark.

"Now, shush."

With some effort, Louisa lifted one end of the weighty door and slid it back in place as best as she could. With Rolf half-heartedly trailing behind, she entered into the passage. Louisa led them along the twisting, echoing hallways, moving forward as fast as she dared. Often, she would be forced to tuck into a corner or duck behind an archway to hide from the Nephilim.

She discovered Radicon first. The clever mechanical man had already picked the lock using his snake-like arm and a skeleton key that was disguised inside of his forefinger. It was quite by accident that they found Gendun next. His tiny prison cell was located in a rather awkward place, inside of a nook carved into the wall.

Gendun's cheeks were shiny with tears. "What are *you* doing here?" he asked, visibly awestruck.

"I dare say, young man, we are here to liberate you," Radicon explained.

Gendun eyed the grumbling Wolfhound with suspicion. "Is *he* coming with us?"

"Rolf wouldn't hurt a fly. Not even a fly like you." Louisa crossed her arms. "Look, do you want to get out of here or not?"

"First, tell Rolf that I'm not his chew toy."

Louisa threw up her arms in resignation and then looked Rolf squarely in the eye. "Rolf, this is Gendun.

Gendun this is Rolf. Gendun is my friend—sort of. Do you understand, friend? Now, sit and be very, very quiet."

Rolf cried a little and then sat obediently.

"Satisfied?" Louisa tapped her foot impatiently.

Keeping an eye on Rolf, Gendun nodded.

Swiftly, Louisa untied his hands.

Together, they managed to locate seven more of the prisoners. The time travellers were found in wretched condition but none more than Brünnhilde, who had been transformed from a beautiful young girl into the bulging, warted witch that Louisa had first met at the café.

Lastly, they discovered Adalbert, who was imprisoned in the deepest and darkest part of the dungeon. He was so greyed and frail that his age was indeterminable, and he had to be carried out by Theoderic.

Gendun led them to the gallery where Belthazzar had stored the time machines.

"We must look for Rhadamanthus and my uncle Hignard," Louisa insisted.

The others had escaped with their time machines.

"We are out of time," Gendun pleaded.

"How right you are, Master Gendun." Rogvolod stepped in front of them.

Rolf let out a low growl.

"Clever, clever children. I suppose your plan was to

escape? Well, it was a nice thought."

Louisa panicked when she heard the cocking of the revolver.

"It is the very last thought that you will ever have; I assure you." Rogvolod levelled his gun. There was murder in his eyes.

Louisa sensed a tremor, barely detectable at first, but soon the entire room quaked. A crackling surge of light arched through the air. Rogvolod's gun discharged with a deafening sound that thundered from one end of the gallery to the other. The bullet struck the arch just above their heads, and bits of brick fell to the floor.

Rogvolod staggered forward, staring at his hands in horror. His flesh was blistering. His mouth opened in an attempt to scream, but no sound emerged. Smoke drifted up from his shoulders and off the top of his head. His robe burst into flames. "Death is but a moment in time and time is but an illusion!" he managed to cry through a puff of smoke and then he collapsed.

Rhadamanthus, stripped of his fine hat and exquisite powdered wig, had dropped from a secret compartment located in the rear of his time machine. He was squatting on one knee, staring through the scope of his electric gun.

"Go! 'Tis not safe, you must escape, while you still can," he gasped. "Alas, the time machine has been incapacitated, and so too, have I." Rhadamanthus' ankle was bloodied and swollen. "'Tis here that I shall take my stand."

"No, Rhadamanthus. We are staying with you," Louisa cried.

"Nay, my lady, go now before the dread-bolted Nephilim are upon us. Perchance, destiny will join our paths together once more."

Rolf whimpered. He was crying and pressing himself up against Louisa.

Theoderic might have lifted the dead weight of Rhadamanthus body, but Louisa knew that she and Gendun could not drag him—with his awkward limbs and round midriff—from the fortress on their own.

"We have to go," Gendun said, flatly.

"I'm sorry, Rhadamanthus." Louisa knew that the only way to help him now was for them to escape.

Louisa and Gendun dashed into the passageway, with Rolf at their heels.

"Have at thee, villains!" Rhadamanthus cried. Flashes of lightning from inside of the gallery lit up the corridor as they made their escape.

"It's this way." Gendun led them through the winding hallways, turning in every direction until Louisa became quite baffled and wondered if they were lost.

"Where are we headed?" she whispered.

"Out."

"Gendun, look."

They bent into a shadow and watched a host of Nephilim float past. In dreadful silence, they continued through the torch-lit hallways until finally, they came to three impassable walls.

"It's a dead end," Louisa gulped.

"To some, maybe." Gendun held up a very old looking black key with a peculiar shape to it. "But not for me. It is a stolen city key; a gift from my vile uncle." Gendun fit the key along the border of the iron grating. With a quick flick of his wrist, the lid was unlocked.

"Try and understand, this is for your own good," Louisa called softly as Rolf's worried eyes sank into the gloom. Gendun's belt was looped under the old Wolfhound's forelegs, and they were lowering him into the sewer.

"Good boy," Louisa assured Rolf, as his wiry beard vanished. There was a splash and a wistful groan.

Gendun pulled the iron lid closed above him and carefully locked it shut. The red torchlight flooded over them from the barred entrance above. Rolf stood shivering and staring upwards with his big, sad eyes. Without a word, Gendun vanished into the mouth of the tunnel. Rolf hesitated, stubbornly sitting back on his haunches.

"Courage," Louisa whispered to him. And together,

they entered into the passage.

The sewer was filled with unexplained sounds and unseen things that slid past their ankles. Louisa grasped at the greasy wall to steady herself. Fearing that she would find a fissure in the floor, she advanced one foot carefully and then another. She reached her arm forward and quite by accident; she clasped Gendun's hand.

Little by little, their eyes adjusted. Moonlight gleamed faintly from the air holes that appeared at long intervals along the lonely pathway. Puffs of air drifted down from these inlets, invigorating her just enough to continue.

They came to a point where two passages met, and Gendun stopped to examine the angles of the walls. He explained to Louisa that if the openings were not as wide as the corridor in which he was standing, they should not enter. The narrower pathways would lead them astray. Following the wider corridors would eventually lead them to the banks of the Seine River, where they could make their escape.

They walked along in silence, but for how long, Louisa could not tell. Inside of the labyrinth, time had lost its meaning. The stagnant air and foul-smelling water was suffocating. At one point, she lost her footing and without meaning to, pulled Gendun and Rolf with her into the putrid stream. Covered in the foul mud of the sewer, the three stood and grimly carried on.

There was a second method that Gendun used to navigate his way. If the current was at their heels, he'd explained to Louisa, the passage led downwards. If the current was at their toes, the sewer ran upwards. But, soon the stream was just a trickle along the floor, and it was becoming increasingly difficult for him to tell which way the water was flowing. He was walking very slowly now, with his head stooped close to the ground. When the stream dried up, there was no longer any way to tell the direction that they were headed. It seemed every route he chose led them farther off course. Twice, he backtracked and then stopped where the passage split, until finally, he sank against the wall. The expression in his eyes told Louisa they were lost.

"Funny, it is quite pretty in this part—for a sewer, that is," Louisa said dreamily and brushed her hand up underneath a majestic arch. "The walls look like they belong in a palace, not in a dirty old sewer."

Gendun was suddenly on his feet. He passed his hand along the archway and then crawled across the floor to examine the slabs of granite and the mortar of thick lime. As he stared at the ground, a smirk turned up the corners of his mouth. "We are beneath the Rue Saint-Denis in one of the most ancient parts of the sewer, built by the old kings of France. It's this way."

The stream resumed its flow—deeper now—as they

continued towards the river. For some distance, they were able to skirt the water's edge by walking along a narrow shelf. When this path ended, Louisa had no choice but to step into the putrid current. In places, the oily water came up to her waist. They walked on like this—half submerged—until Gendun abruptly stopped.

"What is it?"

"A sound," he replied quietly, "Like voices."

They stood for a long while, motionless, listening, but there was only the trickle of the underground stream. Finally, they resumed their slow march onward.

"Where do you think we are we now?" Louisa's breath drifted upwards like a ghost.

"I estimate we are beneath the Louvre. Shortly, we will enter the belt sewer, which empties into the Grand. From there, we can reach the Seine."

There was another question that she had wanted to ask, ever since they first met in the café. "Gendun?" Louisa had said it so quietly that he did not seem to hear her at first.

"Yes, Louisa?"

"Do you live with Adalbert?"

"I do. Or, I did. Or, I still do—but oh, it's so confusing."

"Where did you live—before?"

Gendun spread his arms out majestically. "Under Paris."

"You lived inside the sewer?"

"It's not so bad, once you get used to the stink." Gendun pinched his nose, which made her smile.

"Where are your real parents?"

"I don't know," he replied.

"I'm sorry," Louisa said. "For everything," she added. But he made no reply.

"Gendun?"

"You shouldn't be sorry. Everything is my fault," he said, glumly.

"I don't understand."

"I rigged Rhadamanthus' time machine."

Louisa looked at Gendun in disbelief. "It was you, by the pond. I heard your voice."

"Yes."

Furious, Louisa did not say another word after that.

Finally, Gendun broke the silence. "It's typical."

"And what is that supposed to mean, exactly?"

"It's typical of a girl to sulk."

Louisa made a fist. "One more word out of you—you sewer rat—and I'll punch you right in the nose!"

Rolf had worked his way in between Louisa and Gendun.

"I take it all back," Louisa snapped. "Here I am feeling sorry for you. Well, I'm not sorry. Didn't your parents teach you any manners? I suppose they were just like you then—a couple of dirty crooks."

"I wouldn't know."

"Still, there is no excuse for it."

"It's easy to act so proud when you have a warm home to go to, lots of food to eat, piles of new clothes and parents who hand everything over to you on a silver platter."

"What makes you such an expert on my life, anyway?" Louisa stamped her foot.

"Sorry," he said meanly.

"Well, I suppose you could call that an apology."

"What more do you want? I said it."

"But you didn't actually mean it."

"I'm sorry." Gendun cleared his throat loudly, apparently trying to compensate for the fact that his voice had cracked a little. "I tried to warn you..."

In the passage ahead, a light moved towards them like a needle probing a black canvas. Behind the eerie light, a company of Nephilim emerged. Louisa pressed her hands over Rolf's mouth, and they sank into the noxious stream. Seven of the Nephilim gathered together where three passages converged.

"There wasss a noissse," one of them hissed.

"It came from thisss direction," the other answered, raising a dagger-like finger.

One of the Nephilim crouched along the ground.

Its eyes jerked and twitched as it searched the tunnel. "Thisss way, towards the river," the creature hissed.

As the company of Nephilim filed out of the cul-de-sac the light faded, leaving the three of them shivering in the darkness. They continued on through the grey passages until they came into an open gallery.

When Gendun spoke next his voice was laced with fear. "We have reached the Grand Sewer, but the Nephilim will be waiting for us near the Seine, and we can't risk going back in the direction we came. We must enter the Montmartre sewer, where it will be easy to lose our way."

Louisa's eyes dropped, and a wave of despair came over her. She had heard tales from Grandpa George, of workers who had strayed inside of the Montmartre sewer and never found their way out again.

Gendun examined each entrance along the massive arcade until he found the one that he was looking for. "It's over here," he called to Louisa, though he did not sound keen to enter.

Inside of the passage, the water quickly began to rise. Her foot sank, and the water bubbled up past her knees. With every step, the mud thickened and pulled her a little deeper, until she waded in up to her waist. The mud worsened still, and she sank up to her armpits. But she could not turn back.

"Rolf!" came Louisa frightened voice. "Gendun, wait! Rolf is gone!"

"We can't stop," Gendun insisted.

"I'm not leaving without Rolf."

"Then you will both drown." Gendun took a half step forward, then turned. He struggled back to Louisa and then plunged his hands into the murky water, again and again, coming up with nothing.

"We have to keep searching," Louisa whimpered.

"He's gone," Gendun moaned hopelessly.

"Gendun, come quick, I can feel something!"

Together, they pulled at the wet mound of fur until Rolf's sputtering mouth broke the water's surface.

"Rolf!" Louisa exclaimed upon seeing him. "I thought we'd lost you."

In one last desperate move, Louisa thrust her foot forward. Miraculously, she felt solid ground. She took another step, and another.

The three pulled themselves up and out of the mire and fell to the floor, shivering, coughing and covered in foulness.

"Now what?" Louisa sputtered.

"I don't know." Gendun's eyes made two worried white ovals in the black mud that covered his face.

They had survived the quicksand only to be lost inside of the maze.

∞

Rolf's bottom twitched, and he shook himself from one end to the other, splattering ooze in every direction. He lifted his nose. He had caught the scent of something sweet. He could practically see the delicious smell reaching down into the tunnel like a thin tentacle. He could smell pastries, crepes, macarons and pain au chocolat! There was another scent, something savory this time: a thick piece of roast beef with horseradish, fried onions and gravy. Rolf sniffed some more and then bounded away into the passage.

"Wait!" Gendun called after him, but Rolf was already on his way. "Well, good riddance to you, fleabag."

"Rolf!" Louisa shouted. "For heaven's sake, where are you off to?"

Rolf halted, suddenly concerned for his friends lost behind him in the gloom. The delicious scents had temporarily hypnotized him. He made some very unusual sounds to explain what he had found. Finally, he settled on a sharp WOOF!

"What's gotten into that dumb mutt?" Gendun asked Louisa, but she was already chasing after Rolf, who was shimmying along the passageway with his nose pressed to the ground.

Rolf zigzagged through the complicated passages, following the delicious smells that were getting stronger and stronger. There were voices now drifting down into the sewer. Rolf made one quick glance back at Louisa and then jumped up towards an opening high above in the ceiling.

THE EVENING OF
SEPTEMBER 2nd, 2012

The Grand Palais,

8th arrondissement,

Paris, France

CHAPTER NINE

Out of Time

AN EAR-SPLITTING scream erupted when Rolf, squeezed his whiskered nose up out of the floor drain and emerged a sopping, slimy mess into a pristine marble bathroom. Next, the sewer coughed up Louisa, followed by Gendun. A line of hysterical ladies dressed in couture charged from the toilette shouting, "Monstre! Monstre!"

Louisa eased the door open just enough to have a look outside and then quickly pulled it shut. It seemed they had arrived inside the Grand Palais, and in the midst of a very exclusive fashion show, no less. *Rolf must have picked up the scent of the hors d'oeuvres from a mile away.*

Gendun, who evidently had some experience showering in public washrooms, was standing in the midst of a pile of soiled towels, already clean. His ruined clothes were flung haphazardly into a caretaker's pail, and he was trying on a floor length mink coat that had been abandoned during the mass exodus. "I think there is another one just like it in the stall," he said, adjusting the sunglasses that he'd found in the pocket of his new coat.

Louisa snickered when she caught Gendun admiring himself in the mirror. "I've never seen anything so stupid in my entire life."

"It's not stupid, it's avant-garde," Gendun corrected. "And, if you want to survive in there," he pointed in the direction of the ballroom, "I suggest you get dressed."

There was a polite knock at the bathroom door. "Um, excusez-moi, Mademoiselles? 'Zis is 'ze security." The guard lightly rattled the door. "Allo? Anyone 'ome? 'Zere is a very long line of ladies waiting to, um, make a pee-pee."

Louisa wrenched open the door, and a parade of women pushed inside, filling the stalls and lining the mirrors. She was wearing a brightly coloured turban, long black gloves and a Chinchilla coat that she'd recovered from the bathroom floor. Even Rolf was sporting a pink tutu, and his fur had a gorgeous sheen from the fancy soaps.

Gendun was brushing his hands together in a congratulatory fashion when he came face to face with the incensed security guard, who scrutinized him with his watery St. Bernard eyes. The guard's eyebrows rose in tandem along with the long, slow, deep breath he took upon seeing Rolf. But, before he could utter a word, Gendun snapped his fingers so loudly that the guard's pencil-thin moustache vibrated. "Lapdog," Gendun explained.

Nudging past the security guard, Louisa, Gendun and Rolf stepped into a magnificent ballroom, where the elite of the Paris fashion world crowded. Dozens of crystal chandeliers dangled low over the ballroom from the high vaulted glass ceiling, basking them in a rose-coloured light.

Many a "Yes, darling!" and "You look faaaabulous!" could be heard and everyone was kissing one another on both cheeks, sometimes more than once. Rows of onlookers surrounded a wide runway that spanned the length of the ballroom. A model stepped out onto the runway wearing what Louisa supposed was a dress, but looked more like a spiny, red crustacean. Cameras flashed, and there was a thunder of applause.

"Genius!"

"Brilliant!"

"Bravo!"

Just then, a shadow much quicker than a cloud crossed in front of the moon and a hush fell over the ballroom. Within seconds, the Grand Palais was closed in by a curling fog that crept up the walls and over the spider's web of iron girders and glass. It felt as if the entire building had found its way into the centre of a cloud. Louisa was watching the curious fog, fascinated when a familiar voice caught her attention.

"Fancy bumping into you here, Louisa." It was Hignard, and he was dressed in a tuxedo with tails and a top hat.

"Uncle Hignard, it's you!" Louisa rushed to his side, followed by Rolf, who cried and vigorously wagged his tail at the sight of his master.

"By gum, Louisa, I am glad to see you too. Indeed, I thought you were lost. Why, I thought you were both lost." Hignard was leaning heavily on a cane, trying hard to disguise a limp, but she could tell right away that there was something wrong.

"Uncle Hignard, you're hurt." Louisa took his hand that was damp with perspiration.

"Limping? Fiddlesticks." Hignard was attempting to sound upbeat, but it was clear that he was in pain. "It's nothing, really. Just a bit of old age finally catching up with me. See? No hands." Looking very wobbly, Hignard stepped back from her and raised his cane, nearly toppling over in the process.

"And your face," she cried. "It looks as if you were bitten by a big bug."

The large red lump on Hignard's cheek looked very sore.

"Dear girl, it's allergies, nothing more." Hignard covered the lump on his cheek with a trembling hand.

"Don't you worry, Uncle Hignard, it's going to be all right."

"Thank you, Louisa. You are such a dear, sweet girl. I shall never forget your kindness."

There was something not quite right about the way he was speaking. Every word he said sounded so forced, almost rehearsed.

"Say, I was wondering, Louisa, if you had seen something of mine? It's the funniest thing. I have gone and lost my pocket watch. It is a bit of an oddity, really, not exactly a clock in the strictest sense. It's the hands, you see; they turn in two separate directions at once. Truth be told, it never worked properly from the get-go."

Something flickered in Hignard's eyes, making Louisa uneasy. He had a desperate, almost greedy look.

Hignard is lying.

The lights surged inside of the ballroom. An excited murmur spread amongst the guests when the bulbs began to pop. There was a gasp when the lights cut out, followed by squeals of delight as the ballroom was illuminated once more. It was not long before the bubbly mood turned flat. Strange new visitors had materialized so suddenly it was as if they'd stepped out of the air. They wore long black cloaks that skimmed the ground.

Louisa stepped back from Hignard, who had a monstrous look about him. Desperately, he grabbed a hold of her shoulder.

"I don't have it." Louisa pushed his feeble hand away.

Hignard's head slumped forward, his monstrous expression fading. "I am sorry, Louisa. I don't know what came over me." When he looked up, a change had occurred in him. "Why, I feel as if I had just woken up from a terrible nightmare. I was in a cold, dark place and there was a man with the most unusual eyes and then—" Hignard shuddered. "Take my hand, Louisa," he said, with a surprising assurance in his voice. "I fear we don't have much time."

A gleam of pale gold caught her attention. She hadn't noticed the ring on Hignard's pinky finger until now.

There was a scream, followed by a noise like the splitting of thick ice, and then a crack. A glittering shower of glass fell into the hall. The guests stood frozen, their eyes trained upwards. The Archaeopteryx swooped in through the gaping hole in the ceiling. The bird's massive shadow sped along the floor as he circled over the guests while they scattered in every direction, covering their heads and shrieking as they ran. The beast sent out a piercing cry and plucked a man up in his talons, flying straight up and releasing him. The man howled as he dropped through the air and crashed onto an ice sculpture.

"The girl isss here." The Nephilim stood over the swarm of panic-stricken guests like a grim reaper.

Rolf planted himself firmly in front of Louisa and Hignard. He was snarling and barking wildly at the shadowy men. The Nephilim closed ranks around Hignard and Louisa, hissing and reaching for them with their claw-like fingers. One of the creatures grabbed hold of Louisa's arm.

"Unhand her, you wretch." Hignard brought his cane down onto the awful shifting claw, and the ghoul recoiled. Rolf gave such a vicious bark that the Nephilim halted their advance.

"Jolly good job, Rolf. That's the spirit, ol' chap." Wielding his cane over his head, Hignard stepped towards the Nephilim. "Oh, we've got 'em on the run now, Rolf. Look at 'em turn tail!"

There was a terrifying cry from overhead. The Archaeopteryx fell through the air like a cannon shot, sinking his razor-sharp talons into Hignard's shoulders. With a mighty flap of his wings, the Archaeopteryx lifted him off his feet. Rolf lunged after the giant bird but caught only Hignard's pant leg. With a kick of the bird's powerful leg, Rolf was sent tumbling to the ground. The bird beat his massive wings, stirring up a windstorm that sent tables and chairs skidding across the floor. The Archaeopteryx flew higher and higher towards the jagged opening in the ceiling and disappeared into the dense fog.

"Lou-iiiiis-aaaaa!" Hignard cried as he was sucked up into the night.

A dreadful hissing was coming from the Nephilim as their clawed hands reached for Louisa. And then Gendun was at her side, swinging at the ghastly shape-shifters, who staggered back from his fierce onslaught. But the Nephilim were not subdued for long and advanced on them in lock step.

Gendun turned to Louisa and clasped her hand, but instead of his familiar grasp, she felt cold metal. There was no time for questions. Instinctively, she set to work turning the dials and then, taking a deep breath, she pressed the button. Louisa closed her eyes. There was nothing more for her to do now but wait. There was a deep silence as her heartbeat slowed. The world around her slowed too, then stopped, then fell away.

THE MORNING OF
SEPTEMBER 2nd, 2012

The Grand Palais,

8th arrondissement,

Paris, France

When Louisa and Gendun reappeared in the ballroom, they had returned to the morning that she'd first arrived in Paris. Time had been rewound. The ballroom was empty, the glass roof of The Grand Palais was intact, and all evidence of the chaos had been erased.

"Le fantôme," an old caretaker murmured upon seeing Louisa and Gendun across the dim ballroom. He scuttled away while crossing his chest and sipping from a flask with an unsteady hand.

To the east, a halo of amber pushed back the purple night. The faded moon was low on the horizon, and a few stars still winked in the morning sky. Louisa wondered if far away, in the south of France, another Louisa Sparks was readying herself for a journey. In a few hours, she would board a train bound for Paris, and her adventures would start anew.

"Now what?" she asked, when the bottom rung of a rope ladder dropped down in front of her nose.

"Hunts-up, fair lady!"

"Rhadamanthus!"

"Aye, 'tis me." Rhadamanthus had dropped his ladder through a service hatch on the vaulted roof. He was crouching along an iron girder and craning his neck through the opening. He cupped his hands to his mouth, "Hurry fast, you are not safe. The Nephilim are close at hand."

Only a day ago, if someone had instructed Louisa to climb a rope ladder, some one hundred and fifty feet, to the rooftop of the Grand Palais, she would have outright refused. As it were, she was already halfway up before Rhadamanthus had finished speaking. The cosmic engine hummed and the crystals glowed brightly from the cockpit of the time machine.

"'Tis my good fortune to have found you hither," Rhadamanthus said when Louisa's head emerged through the hatch. "I feared that I had searched for you in vain."

As Louisa stepped out onto the broad glass roof, a gust of wind nearly blew her off of her feet.

Rhadamanthus caught her shoulder. "It does raise my spirits to see you. Alas, the days are wrought with foul tidings. 'Twas with much certainty that I believed you to be taken by the dread-bolted Nephilim! 'Tis only by chance that I have escaped myself."

Rhadamanthus madly leapt around the disorderly cockpit, working the controls, readying the time machine for entry into the wormhole.

"Rhadamanthus, I'm so happy to see you."

"You are too kind, my lady."

"But, I have not been kind, not in the least. I am so ashamed for leaving you like I did. Can you ever forgive me?"

Rhadamanthus tut-tutted, "Not to worry, my lady. We

escaped unharmed; 'tis all that matters."

"When are we going?" Louisa asked as the craft rematerialized into the wormhole.

"Aye, my lady, you speak as a true time traveller. Alas, that question must be answered by you alone." Rhadamanthus lifted the time-scope from his cloak. "Think of an instance that steered your life onto a new path. Change this one thing, and all the things done after it will be undone. Thus, you will never come to know the dark-hearted Belthazzar, and you will be rid of that varlet forever."

"But, then we will never have met."

"Woefully, 'tis true, my lady."

"Will I remember you?"

"Nay, my lady, and woefully I shall not remember you."

His words made Louisa's heart ache.

Rhadamanthus passed her the time-scope. "See what awaits you. The choice is yours."

Louisa raised the time-scope to her eye and was transported to a familiar place.

"Guns be blowed!" the cabby shouted and the car skidded to a halt.

She would only need to delay them for a moment.

"Louisa!" Her father leapt from the cab. "Sweetheart, what are you doing outside? You're not wearing your coat. Run along back home before you catch a cold."

She did not move or speak. She'd dreamt of this moment for so long, but now that it had arrived, she wasn't prepared.

"What's wrong?" her mother asked, kneeling and taking Louisa's hands and rubbing them between her own. "My goodness, sweet girl, you are so cold."

Louisa had never felt anything better in her life.

"Louisa, is everything all right?" her father asked.

Of course, it was. The sound of her parents' voices was the most wonderful thing she had ever heard. She'd nearly forgotten the unique tones that belonged only to them; and the exact way that her mother's hair fell over her shoulders and how her father's eyes radiated with kindness. Their faces were full with concern, their hands full with strength, and their chests full with breath. Her heart was bursting. She had missed them so much.

"My precious girl." Her father rested his strong hand on her shoulder. "We're only going to be away for a few hours."

Her mother wrapped her arms around Louisa, not knowing how long her daughter had wished for that moment.

"None of that, now," her father said, wiping a tear away from Louisa's cheek. "If it means that much to you, your mother and I can stay home."

"Oh no, father, please go. I don't want to ruin your special night. I'm much better now. See?" With all of her resolve, she summoned up a smile. "I'll be just fine on my own."

"Are you absolutely sure, my doll?" Her mother brushed Louisa's hair away from her face.

"Yes, Mum. I'm fine now." She bit her trembling lip, trying to will the words out of her heart. "I just wanted to make sure that I told you... I love you."

"Silly girl, we love you too."

It seemed an entire lifetime since she had seen her mother's sparkling smile.

"I'll tell you what, Louisa," her father said. "Tomorrow is Saturday, and we will have breakfast together with toast and fried eggs and bacon and piping hot tea. And afterwards, we will go to the park to see the giraffes. What do you say? Do we have a deal?"

"Yes, sir."

"Go on home now, darling, before you get chilled." Her mother and father stepped back into the taxicab and waved through the window. And then, for the second time on that very same night, she watched her parents drive away.

When her mother and father arrived home that evening, Louisa was nestled in her bed between Rosencrantz and Guildenstern. She had left the light on in her bedroom, as she often did when she was feeling a bit lonesome.

Tip-toeing into the room, her mother quietly kissed her forehead and switched off the light. When Louisa awoke the next day, Rosencrantz and Guildenstern were waiting for her at her bedroom door.

"Wake up, sleepy head," her mother called from the kitchen. Her father opened the door to retrieve his paper, and a warm, sweet breeze swept into the house. The cold spell had ended.

After breakfast, the five of them went for a walk through Regent's Park, where the wildflowers were already starting to push up through the soil. Rosencrantz and Guildenstern ran off after a butterfly. When she caught up with them, she tucked the flowers she had collected around the edges of their collars and laughed at how silly they looked.

Louisa lowered the time-scope and returned to the wormhole.

"But Rhadamanthus, I swore an oath never to alter the past, and so did you."

"And so too did Belthazzar, but he does not honour it. Alas, even as we speak, the villain Belthazzar plots against us. Think well on what you choose, but do not delay too long, for danger is not far behind us."

Louisa had already chosen; she'd always known the answer. For the first time since the accident, she knew where she belonged.

"I am ready," she said tearfully.

"'Tis the wisest choice, my lady." Rhadamanthus eased one of the levers back. His fingers sped over the console as the time machine entered a loop, traversed its length and then shot out the other side. "There is no other way to escape him."

But, she knew that the time travellers would never be safe until Belthazzar was defeated. "Rhadamanthus, I hope you don't mind that I have decided to stay. My home is in Paris now, and I am a time traveller."

Every line of Rhadamanthus' face seemed to alter, and his skin glimmered with tiny diamond-like particles. "Foolish girl." His waxen smile stretched far too wide, and his eyes twitched and jerked in every direction.

Louisa shrank back. "Who are you?"

His face was melting—reconstructing. "You have something that belongs to me."

"Belthazzar," Louisa breathed.

"I know you have it." Belthazzar caught Louisa's wrist.

She tried desperately to wrench her arm away, but it was useless. Where his hand touched her skin, frost began to spread, and it seemed that ice entered into her veins.

"Insolent child, there can be only one who holds the power to travel through time." Belthazzar's voice was rising higher and higher. "Give me the Parallax!"

"Let her go, Belthazzar." Gendun had two fistfuls of sparking wires, and a stream of smoke poured from the console.

A blast ripped through the cockpit of the time machine and Louisa tumbled to the floor.

"Wretched boy, what have you done?"

"You might say that I've made some simple alterations to the guidance system." With a quick twist, Gendun removed a glass cylinder from the console. "Precautionary measure," he said, tapping the fuse into his pocket.

Another explosion shook the time machine. Louisa tried to catch her breath, but the wind had been knocked out of her lungs. She tried desperately to get to her feet, but the craft was spinning out of control. Her ears rang and her throat burned with the taste of metal. Sparking wires illuminated the tunnel in flashes. She tumbled out of the cockpit into a free fall.

Belthazzar's tremendous voice filled the void around her. "Even death cannot save you from my reach, time traveller!"

Louisa felt Gendun's hand in hers, and she began to shrink.

SEPTEMBER 16th, 2012

The Eiffel Tower,

7th arrondissement,

Paris, France

"I never knew there was an apartment in the Eiffel Tower." Louisa was perched on top of an old metal traveller's trunk that looked as if it had been circling the globe for half a millennia. Outside of the apartment's porthole-like windows, the whole of Paris could be seen from a thousand feet up.

Gendun was sitting in an austere but comfortable looking chair, directly across from her. "Neither does anyone else. It used to belong to Gustave Eiffel until Adalbert won it from him in a card game."

"A good friend once told me, believe none of what you hear, and only half of what you see." Adalbert was looking restored in his best yellow trousers and a plaid waistcoat. Bruce was standing on top of his Homburg hat calling out for his beans!

Hignard was there as well, also decked out in his Sunday best with an enormous crimson peony pinned to the lapel of his jacket. The night watchman had discovered him wandering around the roof of the Arc de Triomphe. "He's a strange bird, that Brucie."

"A *strange* bird, indeed," said Rhadamanthus, who had in fact escaped Belthazzar's dungeon through some good fortune. With a little help from Sigermus, they had narrowly evaded the Nephilim.

Sigermus, along with being a bit of a stutterer, was in reality, quite absent-minded. He was also extraordinarily sentimental and had returned to the dungeon to retrieve his favourite hat—only to discover Rhadamanthus in dire circumstances. He never did get his hat back.

Rolf was watching the automaton circulate the room with the hors d'oeuvres. The Dining and Social Club for Time Travellers was in session.

"Do you think Belthazzar will be back, Sigermus?"

"It is d-d-difficult to say, Louisa. No one c-c-can know for certain what b-b-befell the Atlantean inside of the wormhole. Unhappily, it seems that B-B-Belthazzar is the least of our worries."

Louisa smiled bashfully when Adalbert approached her with a tray of green jellybeans.

"I believe this is yours, Adalbert." Louisa held up the Parallax for him, but he refused to take it.

"I suspect that you will be needing it." His eyes sparkled at the prospect of adventure. "Louisa, there are some things that you must know. It was no coincidence that you found us—"

"Order! Order!" Edward called, striking the podium with his gavel.

The time travellers gave Adalbert a rowdy welcome as he stepped up to the front. "Thank you, Edward. Esteemed time travellers, welcome!" Adalbert cleared his throat and started the meeting in the traditional manner. "The objective of The Dining and Social Club for Time Travellers is for time travellers to dine together," he began. "The Club shall dine on alternate Sundays at 8:15 p.m., punctually." Adalbert looked about the room dramatically. "The identities of the time travellers shall be wrapped in an impenetrable mystery."

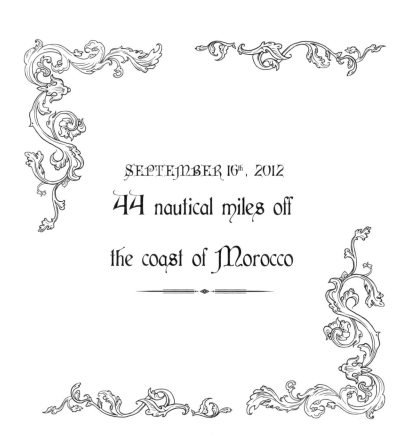

SEPTEMBER 16th, 2012

44 nautical miles off

the coast of Morocco

Far away from the time travellers' spirited meeting, a Chinese cargo ship called The White Tiger, cut through the rough Atlantic waters, off the coast of Morocco. The night watchman stood nervously outside of the captain's quarters, debating whether or not to disturb his superior. Finally, he gave three sharp knocks on the door.

The Radar had detected something unusual to the northwest, less than two nautical miles off the ship's port—something that should not have been there. As the ship continued along its course, the watchman had searched the dark waters. And then he saw it with his own eyes.

"Mhhóu gáau ngóh!" came the captain's voice, which meant, *leave me alone!*

There was an unspoken rule that once Captain Zhou left the bridge, he was not to be disturbed. But on this night, the watchman could not ignore the island with soaring cliffs and jagged peaks that had come, suddenly, bubbling and frothing up from the depths of the ocean. The watchman persisted until the tipsy captain emerged.

"What is it, cadet? This had better be good."

Fin

ELYSE KISHIMOTO

found inspiration for The Dining and Social Club for Time Travellers series through her love of teaching and travelling. She graduated from The University of Toronto with a double major in politics and philosophy and a minor in English literature. She also received a Master's Degree in the Science of Education and has been an elementary teacher in Toronto since 2009.

Q&A with Open Book Magazine, Toronto

OB:

Is there a question that is central to your book, thematically? And if so, did you know the question when you started writing or did it emerge from the writing process?

EK:

The question that is central to the book is: Is our fate decided for us, or do we control our destiny? The debate of freewill vs. determinism is a central theme in Divine Intervention. This question emerged from the writing process and explores how and if the trajectory of our lives can be changed by altering past events.

OB:

Did the book change significantly from when you first started working on it to the final version? How long did the project take from start to finish?

EK:

The project took over a year to complete. The first draft was similar to the finished product, but working with three professional editors gave the book the polish and professionalism that we were looking for.

OB:

What do you need in order to write — in terms of space, food, rituals, writing instruments?

EK:

In order to write I need an open mind, a good dose of adventure, great conversation, and an ever-changing perspective. In terms of tangible necessities, I need a clean counter, a laptop, lots of coffee, and a gym nearby.

OB:

What do you do if you're feeling discouraged during the writing process? Do you have a method of coping with the difficult points in your projects?

EK:

The writing process is full of ups and downs. To cope with difficulties, I take long walks. Getting outside helps to clear the mind. Also, talking things out allows me to come up with ideas and solutions to problems.

OB:

What defines a great book, in your opinion? Tell us about one or two books you consider to be truly great books.

EK:

A great book will keep you up all night, inspire you, teach you something new and transport you to another place or time. The characters don't always have to be relatable, but the story must touch on something personal, believable, and thought provoking.

Oscar Wilde's *The Picture of Dorian Gray* is one of my favourite novels. Wilde is a true wordsmith and creates vivid and compelling characters. The dialogue is clever, witty and eloquent, and often remarks on the most interesting facets of politics, society, and human nature. It is rare to find modern literature with the same level of craftsmanship.

I also love Roald Dahl. You can always expect the unexpected in his books, like when the children are eaten by giants in the *BFG*, or turned into mice in *The Witches*. But, the stories are always fun, and captivating and they are even better when read aloud.

Questions for Discussion

Level 1
1. Where does the story take place?
2. What does the author make you curious about? Why?
3. How does Louisa change throughout the novel?
4. What are Louisa's most important personality traits?
5. Who controls Gendun's actions? How does this make him feel or react?

Level 2
1. Describe the relationship between two characters, their history together, and the significance of their relationship.
2. What would be "out of character" for the main character? (In other words, what would Louisa never do?)
3. What is Belthazzar's plan and what motivates him?
4. Rhadamanthus tells Louisa, "'Tis oft' the smallest alterations giveth rise to strikingly great consequences." What does he mean by this?

Level 3
1. Does the author use humor, irony, symbolism, or metaphors? Give examples and explain the effect.
2. Give examples and explain the purpose of any special language used, (dialects, slang, etc.) and describe its effect.
3. What did you learn from this novel?